Last Fall

Last Fall

BRUCE STOLBOV

89957

DOUBLEDAY & COMPANY, INC.

GARDEN CITY, NEW YORK

1987

All of the characters in this book
are fictitious, and any resemblance
to actual persons, living or dead,
is purely coincidental.

Library of Congress Cataloging-in-Publication Data

Stolbov, Bruce.
Last fall.

I. Title.
PS3569.T6225L3   1987   813'.54   86-24398
ISBN: 0-385-23028-1
Copyright © 1987 by Bruce Stolbov
All Rights Reserved
Printed in the United States of America
First Edition

In memory of
Lynn Barry

The Tribe

HSORO—the introspective leader.
RUU—an extroverted, independent woman and mate of Hsoro.
RHAE—the respected old woman and mother of Ruu and Krilu.
KRILU—a brash young man, hunter.

BRODA—a crippled, but still active, old hunter.
TRARO—the master hunter, friend of Hsoro, and son of Broda.
MRE—artisan, mate of Traro, and sister of Sra.
CLATA—the teenage son of Traro and Mre.
two girls—daughters of Traro and Mre.

KLENA—the old shaman, spiritual leader.
MEKLA—the future shaman and son of Klena.
SRA—cook, mate of Mekla, and sister of Mre.
TYA—the teenage daughter of Mekla and Sra.
two boys—sons of Mekla and Sra.

KRU—a "sick" woman, widow, sister of Mre and Sra.
JAMU—a young boy, neglected child of Kru.

JASCHA—the tribal elder.

And God blessed Noah and his sons,
and said unto them,
Be fruitful, and multiply, and replenish the earth.

And the fear of you and the dread of you
shall be upon every beast of the earth,
and upon every fowl of the air,
and upon all that moveth on the earth,
and upon all the fishes of the sea:
into your hand are they delivered.

Every moving thing that liveth
shall be meat for you;
even as the green herb
have I given to you.

But flesh with the life thereof,
which is the blood thereof,
shall ye not eat.

Genesis 9: 1–4

Last Fall

First Day

CHAPTER 1

A frightening crash broke the still night air, and echoed and re-echoed throughout the mountains and valleys. The moon, two nights before full, peeked silently from behind high, thin clouds.

The music of the night, of autumn, and of survival called in the fierce bugling, starting low, rising to a high note, then dropping and ending with breathless, low-toned grunts. Another long, loud bugle responded. The rock-strewn field shook from the deep rumble of stomping hooves and the loud thud of smashing bones. A trio of gangling bachelors gallantly circled the group of alluring females who ignored their advances. Beside their mothers, curious calves stared quietly toward the center. In the center, kicking the hard ground and barking, two elks eyed each other warily. Their antlers, sharpened for weeks on young saplings and weak males, glimmered like polished flint in the moonlight. The fateful final battle of mating season raged.

Silhouetted by the setting moon, the two bulls in their magnificent prime battled for their pride and their harems. The ground trembled as they rushed toward each other. Their antlers met with a crash that wrenched the surrounding silence. Groaning and twisting, each struggled mightily to conquer the other. They pulled back and quickly crashed their large antlers together once more. Following the commands of their ancient instincts, they repeated their onslaughts again and again: a few steps back, heads down but eyes and antlers up, their front hooves digging into the ground as they barked and snorted, then the sudden, furious run, the earth-shaking smash, and the powerful grinding and scraping of their huge antlers.

Both elks stood four feet tall at their shoulders with racks of antlers that doubled their heights. Both were seven feet long with short white tails and pale yellow rumps. Their thick winter coats were lighter above than below. The younger elk with a coat of reddish brown weighed six hundred pounds. The older elk, weighing fifty pounds more, had a gray-brown coat and a stub for a left ear, the rest torn off in a youthful battle long ago.

Their antlers smashed together. Straining their thick neck muscles and wide shoulders, their antlers clattered as they tried to twist each other off balance. They stopped attacking. The older male pulled back. Heavily misted air shot out of their nostrils as their chests heaved. Both were lean and worn from the many hard battles that had led to this. The reddish-coated male breathed more easily, his younger skin firmer. He stomped the ground aggressively and barked at his older enemy. The other elk, conserving his strength, stood calmly, head straight, eyes wide.

Suddenly, the gray elk charged. The reddish elk took the full force of the charge on his antlers, but his front legs buckled. Pounding his strong hooves, the heavier bull drove forward, not giving his foe a chance to secure a hold. On his knees, his neck bent precariously far back, the hooves of the smaller elk churned and groped furiously until they hit a large half-buried rock. He stopped the assault, barely. With antlers locked, they wrestled with all their might. The more experienced fighter hoped to crack the neck of the upstart and quickly end his challenge.

A chilling wind whistled by. The moon, after hovering momentarily on a stark peak, slipped under the horizon. The battlefield plunged into darkness. Deadlocked, the big bull pulled away. The courageous youth rose again and caught another determined charge. This time he stood and, straining and groaning, held his ground.

The older fighter backed off slowly, five, six strides. His eyes never left his rival, but his head drooped wearily. Both were exhausted from the long battle. Hanging from their ribs, their coats glistened darkly with sweat. Steam rose from their backs into the coldness.

The slighter elk moved a stride forward, then another, and another, boldly challenging the other elk to lift his head and fight. Finally, the older fighter lifted his head. The youth charged, keeping his nose and antlers low to the ground. He caught the old bull underneath his antlers, lifting his front legs off the ground. The sharp antlers of the youth, slashing near the neck, pushed closer. The heavier male, digging his hind legs into the dirt and stones, tried to stop the attack, but was thrown back farther and farther, leaving a long trail of deep parallel ruts in the ground. At last, he stopped the assault. The young aggressor charged again. Driven by instinct, he charged and lunged, lashing wildly at his enemy. He charged again, then let up. Both panted hard.

The older elk was tired. Shaking his head, he tried to gather his strength. He turned and looked at his harem. The youth charged. The older elk caught a slashing blow to his right shoulder. He screamed as the pointed antler ripped through his coat and drove hard into his flesh. His blood spurted from the gash. The elder fell, but staggered to his feet, shakily awaiting the continuing fight.

Feeling strong and confident and aroused by his sense of impending victory over his older enemy, the youth, his muscles rippling, sped into battle.

With the next charge, the legs of the old elk collapsed. He let out a pitiful cry as he rolled over on his back. He regained his footing and fled quickly, chased mercilessly by the victor slashing and tearing at his rump, until the defeated champion buried himself in the thickets at the edge of the field.

The young champion triumphantly trumpeted his victory for all to hear. He loudly proclaimed himself the new king, while the old one, painfully beaten, wounded and weary, walked away from his conqueror, away from his family, away from his friends, and into the forest.

Walking carefully, the injured elk searched for a soft, safe place to rest. He stopped and leaned on a young balsam fir tree, rubbing his gash against its resinous bark. From the distance, he heard the howls and yelps of wolves on their prowl. If they caught the scent of his blood, the pack, hungry, determined, and persistent, would nip and menace him until he dropped from exhaustion. He pushed on deeper into the forest, in need, now more than ever, of a place of refuge to hide and rest.

As he hobbled down the mountain, the mood of the forest changed. The stark colors of the night forest, thick browns, dull grays, and deep blacks, swallowed him. A layer of blown pine needles stuck to the sweat on his legs and mane, and slowed the bleeding of his wound. He limped on farther until he found a mud puddle. He settled down into the soft mud. His head to the ground, his eyes half-closed, but with his ear perked up alertly, he rested. His shallow breathing wheezed.

From a high branch of an old pine tree, a great horned owl hooted low and sonorously. His big, bright yellow eyes searched the forest floor. Every tiny movement he watched diligently. From under a laurel bush, a small stirring attracted his attention. He stared intently, then dove off his perch. The lone owl, the great silent hunter of the forest, drifted without a sound through the gnarled branches. Below, he saw the slight rustling of leaves as a weasel, home from her nightly hunt, a dead deer mouse gripped in her teeth, hid her catch near her nest. Only a slight scratching sounded until the sharp talons clawed the side of the prey. A high-pitched shriek was quickly silenced as the pointed beak of the owl pierced the skull of the weasel.

Awakened by the little cry, a big black bear, dug deeply into her den, soon fell back to sleep.

A gray squirrel and a porcupine found the same pine tree to their liking. With his tail waving calmly behind him as if it had a mind of its own, the squirrel skittishly scurried, and jumped, and paused, and scampered, while filling his belly, and then his mouth, with nuts. The porcupine leaned casually against the trunk, presenting any foolish predator with only a back full of quills, as she contentedly gnawed the bark around the tree. Together for tonight, these two unlikely companions prepared for their first winter.

A twig fell and shook the elk from his stupor. He staggered to his feet. Mud covered his mouth. Salt, from the lick nearby, coated his tongue. He felt terribly thirsty and desperately in need of water. He wound his way, by twists and turns, down the steep slope. Breathing erratically, he stopped occasionally and listened for the badly needed water. At last, he heard the welcome gurgling of flowing water. A faint path wriggled its way through the thick underbrush.

The water flowed through a clearing enclosed by three moss-covered cliffs that looked like gigantic, shaggy monsters forever on guard over a tiny, shimmering jewel. A single rock, lying in the middle of the clearing, turned the trickling water toward the edge of a ravine where it seeped down a five-foot bank. This small trickle of water was but the first rising of an underground stream that little resembled the torrent that roared through here after the spring run-off, submerging all but the highest boulders and tallest tangle of saplings around this now quiet, gently bubbling stream.

Three ways led to the stream. From the north, through a narrow cataract and over a large boulder; or from the southeast, up the sharply cut ravine; or from the southwest, where the elk approached the stream, on a slanting ledge halfway up the cliff. The usually sure-footed elk trembled as he clambered out on the ledge. His hooves clomped loudly on the rock. He stumbled and barked fearfully, then regained his footing. Leaning against the cliff, he continued slowly. He stopped, steadied himself, and jumped to the ground.

He lowered his mouth into the stream and lapped up the cool water. It tasted clean and refreshing, and he drank for a long while. After he drank, he eased his aching body into the soothing water. Facing upstream, with one of his antlers leaning against the rock, his eyes slowly closed. Soon, he slept.

CHAPTER 2

The elk awoke into a world of increasing brightness. The sky had grown murky gray. The still morning mist hung thickly around him, blurring the forest and slopes. Gradually, as his eyes adjusted to the light, he saw the familiar shapes of bushes, trees, and boulders. He shook the sleep from his head and stood up stiffly. Over a patch of maidenhair ferns, he lowered his head and pulled up a mouthful. He munched the good-tasting ferns and swallowed. He pulled up another bunch, then stopped. The fronds hung droopily from his mouth. The clearing sounded abnormally quiet. He pricked up his ear to the sound of the click-click of stones tapped together.

Something flew through the haze; its hissing stopped abruptly as it struck his antlers and fell to the ground. Startled, he spit out the ferns. Lowering his head, ripping the air with his antlers, he prepared to battle his unknown foe. He raised his head and loudly bugled his challenge. A sharp, straight object tore through his throat; its point protruded through the back of his neck. He bellowed a painful cry that echoed off the cliffs. He swayed and staggered as his blood gushed down his chest. He lashed the air with his antlers, instinctively fighting his unseen attacker. Another arrow pierced his wounded, blood-caked right shoulder. He reared up high on his hind legs, brayed, and fell over backward down the ravine. The sharp bank slashed his beautiful coat.

As the elk fell, a man, leaning against the rocks of the cataract, unwilling to face the gruesome scene, turned, and jumped over the rocks. Another man followed him. A third man raced in on the southeast ledge. A fourth man leaped from the top of the cliff, landed like a cat, and sprinted across the clearing. As the first man struggled with the powerful elk, the other three threw their bows aside and jumped.

The biggest man clutched the antlers and twisted them hard to roll the elk on its back, while the other two tried to grab the flurrying legs. When the struggling elk finally rolled on its back, the first man, quickly straddling its chest, pulled out a large stone knife. He looked down at the helpless animal writhing underneath him; the deep brown eyes of the elk stared up at him. The man put the point of the knife against the bloodied throat of the elk. Then, he paused for a moment, and in a hoarse voice, said, "I am sorry." He gripped the bone handle of the knife tightly with both hands, took a deep breath, and plunged the knife into the elk. A sickening scream drowned the clearing. The chest heaved and quaked. Blood spurted out, muffling the final, broken cry. The legs kicked, and jerked, and slowed, and stopped. The elk shuddered once, and then lay still.

The taller of the two men holding the legs left to find a carrying pole. The shorter man stretched the hind leg apart. The biggest man, still holding the antlers firmly, propped the head upon his lap. The man with the knife moved to the side of the elk and pulled the broken arrow from its neck and the intact arrow from its shoulder. He knelt over the corpse. His fingers slid down the breastbone. When he reached the softness of the upturned belly, he stuck in the point of the knife. He pulled out the knife and turned his head away from the escaping, foul-smelling fumes. He waited until the fumes stopped hissing. Pulling the belly skin toward himself with the sharp edge of the knife pointing away from the insides, he carefully slit open the rest of the belly. The intestines pushed out. He slipped his hand inside and to the right. Pulling down on the liver, he exposed the diaphragm separating the abdomen from the chest. Reaching up past the stomachs, he cut the diaphragm all around. He pulled down on the heart and, stretching his arm with the knife up in the chest, cut the throat and windpipe. He cut the tendons around the heart and pulled out the contents of the chest. With no more need to hold the hind legs, the short man moved to the side and, untying a leather pouch from his belt, held it open. The liver was cut out and dropped into the pouch. Then the still warm heart. The tendons attaching the intestines to the back were cut. The kidneys were cut out and put into the pouch. The man with the knife crawled to the rectum. Below the tail, he stuck the knife in deeply and cut around the anus. It still remained attached so he crawled back up and cut again from the inside. He pulled out the rest of the intestines and laid them on some leaves. He pulled out the four ruminant stomachs and laid them alongside. He crawled toward the head. He slit the throat underneath the jaw, pulled down on the tongue, and cut it off at its base. He held it in his hand while the big man let go of the antlers and cleaned off a flat rock. The tongue was laid on the rock. The first man stood up and cut the musk glands out of the shanks of the hind legs. Then, he pulled up a handful of damp ferns, rolled the elk on its side, and cleaned out its insides.

He walked to the seeping water and washed the blood off his hands and knife. He rubbed his thumb against the edge of the knife. The edge felt worn. He squatted down, picked up a handful of fine-grained mud, and spread it on a rock. Stooped over, with his weight pressing down, he scraped the edge of his flint knife. He stopped and checked the edge. It felt sharp. He rinsed his knife and hands again. Laying down the knife, he picked up the tongue. The tongue was washed, checked for parasites, and washed again. He laid it down on the clean rock and, after cutting away the bones from its base, sliced the tongue into four pieces.

The taller man returned, carrying a sturdy, eight-foot-long, birch pole. He let the pole drop to the ground as he ran to the elk. He thumped its side and said, "It is a good elk, Hsoro."

Hsoro slit the top of the rumen stomach. The stomach was almost empty. He pushed in the point of the knife and pulled out the ferns. "Krilu, you shot too soon again. You could have cost us the elk. You will carry it with Traro." He tasted a bit of the ferns. They tasted salty and sour.

"Why not Mekla?" Krilu complained.

Hsoro pulled the ferns out of his mouth and laid them on the ground. "Because, Krilu," he answered quietly, "I said so." He emptied the stomach on some leaves and separated the mushy ferns into three piles. He turned and looked past Krilu. "Traro! You shot well, as usual. You shot well, too, Mekla. Come, let us eat."

The other three men walked over to the water and washed their hands. They each picked up a pile, dropped the bitter-tasting ferns into their mouths, and swallowed. Each unsheathed his knife and stuck it into a piece of the tongue. They walked back and squatted around the elk. Hsoro picked up the last piece of the tongue and carried it as he walked toward the elk. He stepped over the stomachs of the elk and sat down beside the others.

Mists from their breathing drifted through the morning coldness. Even with their furry hides wrapped snugly around them, they shivered. The only warmth came from each other and the corpse. They huddled against the elk, its lingering musky odor filled their nostrils. Blood dripped down on their matted hides as they gripped the tough tongue between their teeth and struggled to slice off the meat in their mouths. Each held his stone knife in his right hand, except Hsoro, who held his in his left.

They all looked tired, haggard, and dirty. All were thin from hunger, but with strong, calloused hands, thick forearms, and tightly muscled legs. Their shoulders slumped from a hard life of heavy work and deprivation. Long, straggly hair, the color of dried grass, hung down to their shoulders. Their beards were blotchy and mangy. Their skin looked pallid, almost bloodless, like freshly pulled roots. The skin of their large faces stretched from high cheekbones, into sunken cheeks, and over muscular jaws. Large noses protruded over fleshy lips, their upper lips reaching only to the tops of their dull, blunted teeth. Thick eyebrows outlined their pale yellow eyes.

The eyes of the other men gleamed as they wolfed down the meat, but for Hsoro, his deeply sunken eyes staring down, the food merely nourished him, stopping the hunger for a while. Skinnier than the others, he was a gaunt, emaciated man. His body looked too small for his head. The pain of being the leader showed on his face. The agony of hard decisions had aged him. Over problems that the others did not understand, he thought and worried. Right and wrong fought within him, haunting him. He was the leader reluctantly. Trusted and respected, he could not refuse. But he did not want to be the leader, and often, in his darkest moods, did not want to be alive at all.

Across the elk from Hsoro sat Traro. Their strengths and weaknesses complemented each other so often, and so well, that these two friends belonged together. Traro was the biggest and strongest of the four, almost handsome, and a master hunter. He felt at home in the forest. Life in the forest he understood. The ways of humans often confused him, but to him the ways of the animals were simple and just. They never killed more than they needed. Like them, he killed because he must and killed as they killed, quickly and surely, with cunning more than muscle. Humble and tolerant, Traro rejoiced in the bounty of nature and accepted her cruelty. He ate contentedly.

Beside Hsoro sat Mekla. He was a good man. Kind and gentle, he had kept his small, round belly. It was the belly of a hopeful man.

Though hungry, he was happy to be alive. His beliefs were simple: he believed in life. He chose living with all its thorns and brambles. Refusing easy self-pity, he stayed with his hope, however slim. He looked upon the famine as an opportunity, a test of his well-being, and felt equal to the task. But more, he felt his unity with every living being and it made him full even when his body hungered. Mekla, more than the others, understood a world beyond the stomach and the coldness.

Krilu ate with proud delight. A young man with burning eyes, he was hot-tempered and aggressive. Bragging that he was the natural leader, he often challenged the leadership of Hsoro. Krilu knew that a leader must be strong, forceful, daring; willing to conquer or die, or better yet, willing to send others to conquer and die for his chosen cause. He could not understand why he was not the leader. He could not understand why the others surrendered their manhood to that silent, brooding man.

The others remembered the fire of their own youth and knew that the fire would burn down soon enough. There were no worlds to conquer here, and leadership was a burden, not a pleasure. Here there was hunger and they hoped that, someday, Krilu would be a good hunter.

Traro, Mekla, and Krilu finished eating and wrapped their hides around them. Hsoro ate slowly.

To Hsoro, Krilu said, "It is a good elk."

Hsoro said nothing. The silence grew.

Mekla said, "Poor elk, he was hungry, too. The males are so skinny by the end of autumn, it is amazing they live through the winter. There is little meat on this and we need more meat. There is not nearly enough."

Krilu rubbed his hands together. "We must kill more before the snow falls."

"We must," said Traro.

"We must leave," Hsoro said as he finished eating and wiped his hands on his hide, "we have a long way to go."

Hsoro turned away. He picked up one of the stomachs and cut off a small piece of fat. He laid the fat on the clean rock. Traro walked over to Hsoro and picked up the end of the intestines near the stomachs. Hsoro gripped the intestines. The slippery intestines wriggled through his hands as Traro pulled. The bulges gathered and slid farther down. When they reached the end, Hsoro turned it away from the fresh water and deposited the wastes on the ground. Hsoro and Traro pushed the intestines, stomachs, and throat back into the elk. Traro turned and threw dirt over the wastes.

Hsoro knelt at the spot marked by blood where the elk fell, then stabbed his knife into the ground again and again, digging a small hole. He wiped the knife clean, then turned to the elk. Leaning over it, he cut off its genitals and laid them in the hole. He opened the leather pouch tied to his belt and, feeling among the smooth stones, found one of the acorns he carried. He laid an acorn in the hole, then covered it with dirt. Traro knelt beside Hsoro and they smoothed the small mound.

Mekla untied long strips of rawhide from his belt. He handed three to Hsoro. Hsoro tied together the forelegs and Mekla the hind legs. Traro snapped off the antlers. Krilu brought the pole and held it between the legs. Hsoro and Mekla tied the legs to the pole. Mekla turned, picked up his arrow, and put it back in his quiver. Krilu walked over and picked up the piece of fat. He rubbed the fat over his moccasins to scare away snakes. Mekla tied the pouch with the heart, liver, and kidneys to his belt. He took the fat and rubbed it over his moccasins. Traro tied both antlers to the middle of the pole. He took the fat and rubbed it on his moccasins. Hsoro tied the head of the elk to the pole. He rubbed the fat on the soles of his moccasins and laid it on the rock.

Though fed, the men were weak. It took all four to lift the carcass. Traro and Krilu sagged as the pole settled on their shoulders. They strained under the weight, but steadied themselves. They walked away. Hsoro, carrying the bows and quivers of the bearers, turned and looked around the clearing once more, checking that the hunters carried all that was theirs.

The bluejays already called to one another, taking back the clearing. Other creatures with wanting stomachs would soon come back. A breeze trembled the leaves and a few yellow leaves fluttered down. The water trickled quietly down the bank. Hsoro walked away. The clearing again lay peaceful.

CHAPTER 3

Mekla, carrying his bow and quiver, led the men down the ravine. He hummed a tune, making up the melody as he walked. His feet shuffled, his small belly jiggled, his arms swung, even the elk swung to his tune. Mekla made almost any day enjoyable. His smile and sense of humor affected all of them. He liked being in the lead where he could see clearly and his short legs could set a comfortable pace.

The morning light tickled the water as it trickled around scattered stones. The men crossed and recrossed the gurgling stream. The water pushed above their knees and splashed the back of the elk. Over rocks, the stream churned noisily, then flowed quietly back to rippling water. Farther along, boulders bumped and tossed the clear water, shaking it suddenly white, then beyond the boulders, the stream lay down and quickly flowed clear again. The men crossed on an old, decaying spruce tree that trembled precariously between two banks. The dancing stream rushed down the mountain; the tired men turned and headed up the mountain.

The stream grew. Flexing its foaming muscles on decomposing trees, it rumbled over eroding boulders. It dove and dug its watery strength through the sheer granite walls. Its roaring drowned out all other sounds. Its spray kicked up. High above, a ledge, cut into the canyon by the stream at the height of its spring flood, served as a faint path for the men.

Damp pine needles on gravel eroded from granite covered the path. Green and brown lichens grew on the craggy face of the granite, while dried deerhair rush withered on the hard ground. The men wriggled around boulders and stunted red pines that gripped the rocky ledge. The path zigzagged up and into the shadow of the mountain.

The men trudged up. Their feet pounded on the stiff rock. The ground grew more barren, the path became harder. Hearts thumped against chests, chests felt tight, breathing came hard. Sweat dripped down their faces. The path stopped. The men stopped and stared with quiet helplessness at the rocks blocking their way.

Hsoro said, "Mekla and I will stand on the ledge above. You lift it to us."

Hsoro and Mekla climbed up the rocks to the small ledge. They laid down the bows and quivers. They dug their feet into the loose gravel.

Traro asked Krilu, "Are you ready?"

"Of course, I'm ready."

Traro tightened his grip on the pole. He dug his feet into the gravel and said, "One, two, three, LIFT!"

Traro and Krilu lifted the elk up and onto the bent shoulders of Hsoro and Mekla. As they struggled to steady the pole on their shoulders, a stone under the foot of Mekla slipped. Mekla slid to the end of the ledge. He screamed as the elk swung out over the edge. Traro dove at the elk, driving his shoulder into its side, slamming Mekla and Hsoro against the rocks, knocking them all to the ground. His scream still echoed through the canyon as Mekla breathed a long sigh of relief. A grin brightened his face. He rested his face on the rump of the elk and said, "Aren't we a pretty pair?"

Traro laughed and Mekla chuckled, slapping the side of his belly. Laughter covered the men.

"Mekla and I will carry it to the top," said Hsoro. He leaned over and patted Traro. "Thank you."

Traro and Krilu, carrying the bows and quivers, followed Hsoro and Mekla up.

From the top of Far Mountain, their world opened before them. The mountains looked like slumbering furry creatures exhaling the dew, their backs jutting up from the haze. Awakening eyes of lakes, blanketed in mist, looked up from the sleepy valleys. Rising in all directions, the mountains appeared colder, darker, more gray, as they faded into a long, undulating, indistinguishable horizon.

Hsoro searched the horizon. Though more vital thoughts nagged him during this autumn of sharp thunder, he still wondered if there was anyone else. He never failed to look for any sign when he reached the top of a mountain. He never found anything. For a long, long while, they had been alone.

The sun peeked over the mountains and gradually climbed. It gripped the darkened silhouette, stretching itself, holding on for one more moment, before leaving the earth. Long, gray clouds, in the brightening familiar blue, floated above.

Below, a smoky haze covered the evergreen forest of Summer Valley. Twisting through the forest, Walking Stream curved at the far end of the valley around the base of White Mountain before tumbling into Winter Valley. In the center of Summer Valley nestled Teardrop Pond.

Willow trees bordered the shore of Teardrop Pond. North of the pond, a pale yellow meadow of goldenrods opened around Walking Stream. Away from the stream, next to the meadow stood a large oak tree. Beneath the tree, barely visible from so far away was a small clearing. Home.

CHAPTER 4

With Mekla again in the lead, Traro and Krilu carrying the elk, and Hsoro behind, they started toward home.

The path curved around the top of the peak through a patch of gnarled, wind-stunted thickets, and then plunged down. Bounding over abrupt grassless gullies, hurtling through tight turns strewn with pinecones, bending low under drooping branches, jumping over damp upright roots, they rushed down the mountain.

"Whee!" shouted Mekla.

The bulky elk swung wildly from side to side and Traro grabbed it.

Alternating stripes of sun and shade made the bodies of the men flicker, larger in the light, smaller in the dark, as deeper into the glen they ran. The wind raced through the treetops. The diminishing notes of a canyon wren whistled through the trees. Ricocheting off branches on its way down, a cone fell from a pine, hit the ground, bounced, and plunked into the stream. The sounds of the wind, woods, and water blended together.

The stream fell, bursting down, then rumbled away. Cascading around mossy boulders, the stream created a moist world of overgrown vines and bushes, decaying trunks, and pungent smells. Behind rocks, the water rested. Crinkled ferns, twisted needles, and dead leaves, all casualties of the coldness, covered the calm pools.

The men, soaked in sweat, stopped. Mekla lay down on his stomach, plopped his face into the cool water, and drank. Krilu watched as his spit oozed down the furrowed bark of a fir tree, mixing near its roots with the moss soaked by his urine. Traro stood still, a mud dauber wasp buzzed around him. He watched the insect as the sun flickered on its iridescent body, turning it blue for an instant, then green, then purple. Traro smiled at the beauty of the stinging creature.

Next to a blue spruce knelt Hsoro. A ray of sunlight, streaking through the branches, brightened a dewy cobweb. The lacy, translu-

cent web of an orb-weaver spider glowed in the light. He stared at
the artistry of the delicate, premeditated structure as a fly flew unwit-
tingly into it and stuck to its sticky tangles. Quickly, from its roost in
the corner, the spider scurried down. In an instant, it wrapped the
struggling fly in imprisoning silk. As the fly twitched desperately, the
spider calmly sucked the life from it. Hsoro turned away; and the
others followed.

The squish of their own footsteps in the mud accompanied the
men as they waded through the marshes. The pole creaked. A gray
mist grazed against the scalloped shoreline and hovered over the
dark water. Teardrop Pond lay shrouded in early morning silence.

A group of mallard ducks cruised on the vapory water. Some
dunked their heads underwater with their webbed feet sticking into
the air, then popped up, with their bills filled with brown algae.
Others munched on the free-floating duckweed. A stone hit the water
by one of the ducks, skipped over her head, and hissed into the water
near the men. The duck ran upon the surface of the pond flapping
her wings. The other ducks squawked and scattered and squawked.
She tucked her legs and glided into the water. The ripples widened
and faded. The pond slid back to silence.

Pale gold leaves of willow trees fluttered down and stopped
abruptly when they touched the water. One spun completely around
as if its life was not yet over, then stopped. Leaves covered the shallow water and piled along the shore. The ground grew solid under
their feet and the soothing, rhythmic plashing of water murmured
softly in the ears of the men as they carried home their prize.

A large black willow tree bent over the pond. Underneath it, leaning his back against its trunk, a ragged old man held a long willow
fishing pole. He sat as still as the ground and as unmoved as the
roots.

A spindly old man, wearing only a loincloth, stood knee-deep in
the water. In front of him, two rows of protruding willow sticks,
pounded into the mud and lashed together, spread like a gaping
mouth toward the currents of the pond. The two rows of sticks
narrowed into an enclosure of thigh-high sticks that widely encircled
him. In his left hand, cocked near his ear, he held a long spear. Its tip
pierced the surface of the water. As if trapped himself, the man
stood, frowning and staring down into the water.

"How is the fishing today?" shouted Traro.

"Nothing!" the man facing toward the pond answered gruffly. The man in the pond spoke softly, "It would take great luck—" "—or a dumb fish—" "—to catch anything when the pond is turning over." He shook his head as he stared down.

The other man lifted his fishing pole. The milkweed line pulled up a short piece of bone sharpened at both ends with a dragonfly tied across it. The bait was untouched; the gorge empty. With a flick of his wrist, the man threw the gorge far out into the pond. "But I am a crippled old man and can do nothing better than to try to catch fish. Damn dumb fish!"

"Father," Traro said, "fish are not dumb. They are smart enough not to want to be in your grumpy belly. Come! Skinning our catch may fit your mood better."

"Damn dumb fish!" Broda dug the end of his fishing pole hard into the ground. He grabbed his crutch, tucked the broad end under his right shoulder, and hobbled toward the men. Below his right knee, the leg of his breeches, flapping loosely in the breeze, hung empty.

Shouting and screaming filled the air. From over a knoll, women and children, waving and yelling, ran toward the men. Mekla jumped up and down, wigwagging his arms excitedly. Krilu whooped triumphantly. A tumultuous celebration crushed the quietness. Women cried. Children laughed. Men cheered. Giggling children raced around, drumming the sides of the elk, singing, "Skin and bone! Flesh and meat! Food to eat! Food to eat!" Impromptu dancing burst out. Friends put their arms around each other and patted their stomachs.

The crowd quieted as one by one they noticed an aged man walking stiffly toward them holding the arm of an old woman. The crowd stepped aside as the man walked forward with small, hesitant steps. The woman led the man to the elk. He slid his hand over the elk as he walked around it. He stopped and slid his hand down its back until he crouched nearly to the ground. Leaning against his cane, he slowly straightened himself to his full height. The bent, little man suddenly appeared noble. He nodded slightly to himself. A small smile unfolded on his deeply wrinkled face. The tribe roared in unison. Dancing and laughing started again. The elder and the old woman turned away, walked up and over the knoll, and disappeared.

The Tribe followed. Sounds of people faded away, leaving Hsoro alone on the shore and the old man standing in the water.

"How many fish, Klena?"

"You do not have to ask. The fish are ready for winter. They do not care to please an old man with a spear and an empty trap. We have all the fish we are going to get. It is not nearly enough."

"Not nearly enough," Hsoro repeated as he slumped to the ground. His hide dropped from his shoulders. He stared across the suddenly empty-looking pond.

Dead leaves stuck to the soles of his feet and water dripped off his pale legs as Klena sat beside Hsoro.

Hsoro asked, "Are you ready for the Ceremony?"

"I will be ready and the Ceremony will be performed." Klena dug the end of his spear into the ground and, holding it with both hands, leaned his shoulder against it. He gazed over the water. His eyes did not look at Hsoro, or, it seemed, anything else of this world. "For fifty years, we have kept the Ceremony, and for the last twenty-five, I have led it. This will be my last. It is time to pass my duties to my son Mekla. I am too old."

Hsoro turned and stared at the familiar profile of Klena. He saw a calm face, furrowed, with a wispy white beard stuck to his chin and jaw. Thin, almost invisible hair lay far back from a high forehead. Thick eyebrows hung like full branches over deep-set amber eyes. Yet, only Hsoro saw agelessness.

"You have been the shaman since I was a boy. When my parents died, you raised me as your son. Klena, you are not too old. You are just tired and hungry. We all are."

Klena leaned his cheek against his spear, rubbing the small scar on his forehead as he always did when thinking deeply.

Hsoro felt a hand on his shoulder. He turned. "Ruu!"

She offered her hand and they walked, together, toward the knoll.

Her long hair, light with a tint of deep gold, flowed freely around her shoulders and breasts. She had strong arms and large hands that swung easily at her sides. Her muscular legs and calloused feet moved confidently over the ground. The skin of her taut body possessed a darker, earthy hue. Her nose flared as she breathed in her world. Her eyes glowed brightly. In a husky voice, she said, "The hunt went well."

"Yes, but—" His voice choked.

"It's a large elk."

"Not nearly enough," Hsoro muttered.

"It's good to have you home," Ruu said.

She and Hsoro had mated nine summers ago. She chose Hsoro, and he, always the loner, consented. His intelligence, his intenseness, and his eyes, those almost infinite eyes, attracted her. She felt that Hsoro, sensitive and kind, would not only lead the Tribe, but, with her urging, would shape them. She dreamed of a Tribe free from the daily struggles for existence and the daily terrors of starvation. No longer would they be a pitiful group on the brink of extinction, but a Tribe, happy and prosperous, secure in its present, sure of its future. Working with Hsoro, she felt certain that her dream would come true.

Hsoro leaned against a rock and vomited down its other side. He spit to clear his mouth, turned around, and leaned his back against the rock. He was deathly pale.

"You're tired," Ruu said, standing beside him with her arm around his shoulder. "I'll make you some sassafras tea and then you must rest."

"Why cannot meat fall like rain from the heavens? Why must we live by killing? Always, always it is death that we bring. Death and pain. Must we kill or starve? Is slaughter our only gift to this world? Is this why we are here? Another carcass and another and another and always it is not nearly enough! I feel sick! I cannot stand it, but I have no choice. I have no choice! Oh, why was I given this hole in me that demands daily sacrifice? What kind of questions are these? I do not know. I wish we never had to eat at all!"

"But we must eat. You're tired. You need sleep."

"Food! Damn, damn food! Is that all there is? Is that all we are here for? Always it is food! Awake, it is food. Asleep, it is food. I dream and it is food!"

Ruu put her arm around Hsoro and helped him home.

CHAPTER 5

Near the knoll, Traro and Krilu stopped and bent down, and the back of the swaying elk touched the logs on the ground, then stopped. The men groaned as they took the pole off their sore shoulders. Krilu yawned as he walked away.

Traro pulled the pole from between the legs of the elk. The elk rolled on its side. Its intestines, stomachs, and throat spilled out. Its legs pointed toward the five children sitting quietly in front of the logs. They stared at the elk, and at Traro as he untied the antlers from the pole, laid them in front of the logs, and walked away. Klena walked over the knoll. Broda leaned on his crutch over the elk.

Broda held a large stone knife, and in his other hand, a rock. He scraped the edge of the knife against the rock. When the knife felt sharp under his thumb, he laid the rock down.

Broda laid his crutch down and knelt beside the elk. He cut through the skin on the inside of the hind leg, then slit up the skin of the leg. With his other hand pulling it off, he sliced the skin from the flesh with his knife. He turned to the other leg and cut the skin from it. He laid both flaps from the hind legs on the logs. He cut through the rump at its tail, leaving the short white tail on the skin.

He moved to the side of the elk and shook his head as he said, "There is not nearly enough fat on it."

"And only enough meat for seven days," Klena said as he knelt beside Broda.

"We must make it last ten," Broda said.

Klena nodded in agreement as he grabbed the skin with both hands and peeled it away. He pulled slowly and steadily as Broda crawled beside the elk cutting the skin from the flesh. The skin peeled off smoothly.

A tiny piece of meat stuck to the skin. Broda cut it off and tossed it to the waiting children. The children shouted as they tried to grab the piece of meat from each other until they saw Klena glaring at them. They sat down quietly and the meat was given to the youngest child, a boy named Jamu. He quickly dropped the meat into his mouth, patted his stomach and sighed contentedly, while the other children stared eagerly at Broda.

Broda and Klena stopped at the shoulders of the elk. Broda skinned both of its forelegs. Klena peeled again and Broda sliced again. Klena pulled the skin up to the neck and stopped. Broda cut entirely around the neck, then sliced the skin away from the neck as Klena pulled. The skin came off completely. The two experienced men rolled up the skin.

Bracing the stump of his leg against the knee of the elk, Broda snapped off its lower foreleg. Three more times, and all four shanks, with their hooves still attached, lay in a pile.

Broda sliced deeply around the neck of the elk, then stuck the knife in, cutting through its spine. He laid the knife down. He and Klena grabbed both sides of the head, then twisted it from side to side until it snapped off. They held it high for all to see. The entire Tribe stopped. They stared, smiling quietly. Jamu looked up at it and whistled. As Broda and Klena held it up, the last few drops of blood dripped down from the severed head of the elk.

The two old men laid the head down. Broda picked up a large ax and stood. With a loud grunt, he brought its stone head down hard into the backbone of the elk, cracking the carcass in two. Klena cut down the back and laid the halves flat on the logs. With a well-placed blow below the lowest rib, Broda split the half into fore- and hind-quarters. He brought the ax down again, but the other half did not split. He shook his head slowly in disgust. The next blow did not split it either. He leaned against the ax handle, muttering, "Crippled old man." He lifted the ax over his head and slammed it down hard and fast, splitting the half, and shattering the oaken ax handle.

Towering overhead, in the center of the village, stood the oak tree. It stood twenty times taller than any of them. Two adults could put their arms around its trunk without touching hands. Within its wide crown, its stout branches twisted and strained toward the life-giving sunlight. Already, its northern and upper branches were bare. The rest of it was covered with tan leaves that would all turn brown, most would fall, and a few would hang on past the first snowfall.

Mekla climbed up the knobby trunk. Twenty feet up, lashed firmly to sturdy branches on opposite sides of the trunk, were two shacks, one higher than the other. In the lower shack, pebbles lay on the floor, thrown to scare away scavenging crows. The breeze blew a few withered leaves across the floor of the empty shack.

Mekla climbed to the upper shack. By their legs hung the skinned and dried remains of a weasel, a muskrat, two porcupines, and a deer butt. By its neck hung a featherless crow. That was all. Mekla shook his head and said, "Not nearly enough."

He lowered a vine down to his father. Klena tied the vine to a hind quarter. Mekla pulled up the hindquarter, then the other, then a forequarter, and hung them all.

The other forequarter would be eaten soon, so Klena hoisted it up to a lower branch and tied the vine around the trunk of the tree as Mekla climbed down.

The children stood in a circle waiting for Mekla. Ruu had taken Hsoro to their hut. Traro and Krilu had gone to their huts to sleep. Broda and Klena were busy with the messy job of cleaning the head of the elk. The women of the Tribe were hard at work. The children stared pitifully at Mekla. Their large, plaintive eyes emphasized their small faces. They stood with their arms hanging limply at the sides of their skinny bodies. Two boys were the children of Mekla and Sra. The two girls were the children of Traro and Mre. The other boy, Jamu, was the neglected child of the young widow, Kru. Mekla shook his head sadly as he looked at the children standing around him.

Lifting his small son to his shoulders, Mekla took the hand of his older son and waved for the rest to follow. He took them away from the village to a place under a pine tree where the ground was soft with needles. All the children sat down and looked up at Mekla.

"Long ago, there was a bear, a big brown bear, much bigger than me." Mekla stood as tall as he could, high up on his toes with his arms stretched over his head, imitating the bear by growling at the children. He bent down until he was nearly as low as the children and said, "But this bear did not like how he looked. He thought his head was too flat and his fur was too dull. He would sit all day in the sun and comb his fur with his paws. He tried rolling in the sand to make his fur brighter. He tried rubbing against sticker bushes to make his fur longer. He tried just about anything to make himself look better because he did not like how he looked." The children smiled as Mekla acted out all the things the bear tried.

"Well, the bear somehow got it into his thick head that the only way he could be beautiful was to wear clothes. So, he got a raccoon cap and a mooseskin robe and deerskin moccasins and started wearing them. Soon, he added more and more clothes until he had rabbit-fur gloves, a weasel scarf, mole earmuffs, and even a pinecone necklace. He thought he looked absolutely splendid. Everywhere he went, the other animals he met said how different he looked, or how interesting his clothes were, or how they made him look like nothing they had ever seen before. When he would strut through the forest on his hind legs with his chest out and his paws swinging daintily in the air, the other animals would just smile and shake their heads or giggle quietly into their paws." Mekla acted all this out, adding wiggling hips to the image of the bear. "Only the bluejays laughed, but the bear thought they were crazy anyway, because they laughed at everything." All the children laughed like bluejays until the noise grew so loud that Mekla, to quiet them, put his finger over his mouth. "Shh!"

"One day, near the dam of the beavers, he was walking high up on his toes, trying hard not to get his pretty moccasins muddy. A young beaver, working hard on the dam, saw the bear, at least he thought it was a bear, but he had never seen anything quite like this strange-looking creature. He stared for a long while, for beavers do not have very good eyes, until he was sure that it was indeed a bear. But the sight of the bear wearing clothes made him giggle. He could not stop himself and he started to laugh and laugh. More beavers came out and, when they saw the strange-looking bear, they began to laugh and slap their tails loudly on the water. The bear growled, 'Don't you know who I am?' The beavers just pointed at him, laughing and rolling themselves into giggling, furry balls.

"Soon, all the animals in the forest were laughing and giggling. The owl, the toad, and the crow, all friends of the bear, laughed, too. They knew that he had looked silly, but had been too afraid to tell him. The confounded bear could not understand what they were all laughing about. He adjusted his earmuffs, took his scarf and wrapped it graciously around his neck, and walked to the edge of the pond. There, in the water, he saw the most incredible sight he had ever seen. He leaned over for a closer look, then jumped back in surprise. 'What was that?' he asked himself. He crept cautiously back to the pond and looked in again. This time there was no mistaking the silly-looking creature reflected in the water. 'I look like a fool!' he growled. He was very embarrassed. He threw off his gloves and pawed off his clothes, ripping and tearing them to shreds. When they were all off, he jumped up and down, stomping them into the mud, rippled his muscles, and roared loudly.

"On his way home, he saw his old friend the owl. 'Why didn't you tell me I looked so foolish?' he asked. The owl turned his head from side to side and hooted, 'Who, me?' Later, he asked his friend, the toad, who was hopping by, and the toad croaked, 'Why, me? Indeed!' The old crow, flying overhead, simply answered, ' 'Cause!'

"Early the next morning everyone was awakened by the sound of a large tree crashing down. It shook the whole forest and scared many of the animals. They searched for what made such a loud noise. Soon, they saw the bear walking to the pond with a tree in one paw and a honey-filled hive in the other. All that day, the bear knocked down trees, dragged them to the dam, and shared his honey with the beavers.

"And so, children, the bear, after trying to be something he was not, was happy to be just a bear, and from that day on, he tried to be the very best bear he could be."

The children clapped and smiled. Mekla stretched and yawned. His sons imitated him. Mekla smiled and said, "I feel sleepy, I'll see you later." He waved as he walked back to the village. All the children smiled and waved at him.

CHAPTER 6

The village huddled against the bottom of the shady, southern slope of Broad Mountain. Like vigilant guards, to the east of the village grew the woods of gold-leaved birches and aspens with their shimmering shield-like leaves. To the south of them stood a lone pine with the children, playing catch with a pinecone, under it. Bordering the southern edge of the village at the meadow stood a three-foot-high stone wall, extending from the pine to the knoll west of the village. Rising from the meadow, the knoll, the same height as the wall where they met, leveled off beyond the wall, then rose again and joined Broad Mountain. A few scarlet-leaved maples grew at the base of the slope behind the village before giving way to a mountain of evergreens.

Two long-limbed maples leaned languidly over two dilapidated huts. Back and away from the commotion of the village were the huts of Broda, nearest to the knoll, and Klena, farther along the base of the mountain. Nestled farthest back in a protected nook, where two old pines sheltered it from the weather, was the well-kept, sturdy little hut of Jascha.

In front of these huts was a clearing. For ceremonies and tribal councils, the Tribe would gather, here, at the Ground.

Built to the east of the Ground, and the hut of Jascha, was the small, well-kept hut of the old woman Rhae. To the south of her hut was the larger but poorly kept hut of Ruu and Hsoro. The hut of Ruu's brother, Krilu, better built but dirty, was near the stone wall to the east of a larger clearing called the Hearthland. To the west of the Hearthland, nearest to the knoll, was the hut that the teenage son of Mre and Traro, Clata, had built himself in the spring. Near his hut were the logs used for butchering, cleaning hides, and other chores needing a clean surface. Next to the logs, nearer the wall, a square enclosed by stones held black walnuts, drying in the sunniest place in the village. Next to that, at the wall, was a low mound of dirt. An opening divided the wall in the middle and a well-worn path showed how often they used it. Between the opening and the mound was the hearth, close enough to the wall to protect the fire from the wind but far enough away so the Tribe could stretch out comfortably and relax around its warmth while their meals cooked.

Between the Hearthland and the Ground, and between the knoll and the oak, three huts stood in a row. Nearest to the knoll was the large hut of Mre and Traro and their two young daughters. In the middle was the largest hut in the village, the home of Sra and Mekla, their two sons, and their teenage daughter, Tya. Next to the oak was the strongly built storage hut. On the other side of the tree was the small, neglected, nearly collapsed hut of Kru.

"Mekla!"

Mekla continued tiptoeing past the hut of Kru, but not quietly enough.

"Mekla!" Kru tossed a wooden bowl out of her hut. It rolled over his foot and stopped in front of him. "I'm thirsty. My bowl is empty. Bring me water!"

He stopped and his shoulders slumped. His face grew tired. He looked forlornly to his mate Sra, sitting in front of their hut.

"I will get it for you, Kru," Sra said, smiling at Mekla.

Mekla ran over, hugged Sra, and kissed her on the lips. "Thank you," he whispered, then crawled into their hut.

Sra laid down the stone she held in her hands. She lifted the flat rock in front of her and poured another load of finely ground acorn flour into a large woven basket, filling it. She stood up, took the basket, and balanced it carefully on her head, holding the edge of the basket with her right hand. She leaned over, picked up a clay jug with her left hand, and held it against her hip as she walked into the meadow.

In the morning light, the goldenrods in the meadow looked old and tired, past their peak, fading to brown. Swarms of black and yellow bumblebees and long, spindly mosquitoes gorged themselves with nectar and blood before winter. Much fainter now than in summer was the humming of the insects as they died by the millions every day, unnoticed. Of the hordes of butterflies that had flown south in the past few weeks, only a few were left, shivering on the flowers. Beside the stream, a pair of busy frogs filled their bellies with mosquitoes. Sra was preparing for winter, too, filling basket after basket with acorns, grinding them into flour, and baking bread before the Tribe left for the Winter Cave.

Baskets filled with acorn flour being leached of its bitter tannin lay in the stream. After the long, hard task of grinding the sun-dried acorns, Sra poured the flour into baskets, weighed the baskets down with rocks, and laid them in the stream for one day to wash out all the tannin and make the meal edible. She pulled a basket out of the stream and put the basket she carried in its place. After filling the jug, she stopped over a still pool and looked at herself.

Sra was not pretty but she had grown to like how she looked. Her face was plain and thin but there was nothing she could do about it. She smiled at her reflection as she thought about how much Mekla loved her and it made her eyes sparkle. She loved Mekla and their three children. With them, all her work felt worthwhile. She knew their lives were hard, but she felt they lived in a beautiful world and its simple joys filled her life.

Rhae, describing her, said that Sra's heart bubbled. When Sra heard this, she felt warm inside. She was kind and friendly, good-natured and gregarious. She liked to talk, and to listen, too. To her, conversations were great fun. People opened up easily to her. It made them feel better to talk to her about their problems, and she was appreciated as a patient listener. She rarely gave advice, for people rarely follow the advice of others. They had to find their own way, and she preferred to be a good friend and liked, rather than a respected adviser. When talking to her, people thanked and hugged her when all she had done was to listen with an open heart while they thought out loud. As she listened, she learned, more than most imagined. She learned to listen to the problems of others instead of scurrying about causing problems for others.

"Bring me my water!" shouted Kru.

Sra hurried back to the village. Water splashed out of the jug and dripped down on her legs from the basket of leached acorn flour. She filled the bowl with water, slid it inside the doorway of the hut, and walked away.

"I cannot reach it!" shouted Kru.

Shaking her head, Sra took the basket to her older sister, Mre. "This will take me a while," she whispered, putting down the jug, then turned and walked back to the hut.

Mre watched Sra crawl into the hut. She shook her head, too, then turned and looked at the basket in her lap. She leaned close to the basket and squinted at it. She remembered every weave of it, every time the reeds ran out before she planned, every mistake she made and fixed, or could not fix. She remembered how hard she worked to weave it tight enough so the flour would not fall through. Mostly, she remembered how glad she was when she finished it. It took so long to make, but she could not hurry it. It grew at its own pace, with a life of its own. Rhae said that Mre made things come alive. Mre smiled when she heard that because these things were already alive before she made them. Mre liked making baskets, but more, she liked getting better at something, feeling that something grow in her hands, and finally, seeing it finished. She lifted the basket and frowned at a mistake she had tried to fix near the bottom. The rest of the Tribe admired her handiwork and told her that she was very good. She knew she was not very good, but she was getting better.

Mre wore her hair tied back. She was a stoutly built woman with a serious face and a slight softness at the corners of her eyes. She had an inner glow that could be felt more than seen. She showed it with her gentle touch, soft voice, and bright eyes. It came from a contentedness with her life, with her beloved Traro, and with their family. Whether it was making baskets, pots, clothes, acorn bread, or loving Traro and their children, Mre filled her life with beauty.

She leaned over the basket of leached acorn flour in her lap. She always enjoyed the feel of the dough in her hands. Concentrating on how it moved as she kneaded it, she said, "It moves so much like clay." She stopped, tapped her forehead with the back of her hand, and said, "I must add the clay." She added a pinch of clay, one part for every twenty parts dough, to make the bread rise. She always thought it strange for clay to work that way, but she accepted truth without always understanding it. When she finished each loaf, she patted it flat on top and drew a small butterfly on it.

Sra returned and sat next to her sister. She looked at the loaves with the butterflies on them and said, "The butterflies are almost gone, but they were so beautiful."

"It is so beautiful how they fill the sky with wave after wave of oranges and blacks," said Mre as she wrapped each acorn loaf in leaves. "Yet each butterfly is such a delicate, helpless-looking creature. It is amazing that they can fly over mountains. How many more mountains must they fly over until they find their homes? Year after year, they delight and humble us with their struggles. So beautiful and so strong."

Sra sighed. Her mind wandered off with the butterflies and back to the joy they brought to Mre and herself. She loved listening to her sister.

"How is Kru?" Mre asked as she continued wrapping the loaves.

"I cannot find what is wrong with her," said Sra, sadly shaking her head. "She looks pale and tired, but no more than all of us. We are all tired, but we keep working because we must. She lies in her hut with her back to me. When she does talk, she complains. I cannot find what is wrong. I want to help her," her voice tailed off as she pushed a wisp of straggling hair behind her ear, lowered her head, and began again to grind acorns.

CHAPTER 7

Ruu sat cross-legged on the logs with the skin of the elk in her lap. In her left hand, she held a rock and scraped the edge of her knife against it. She checked the knife against her calloused thumb. The edge felt sharp. Gripping the knife in her right hand, she picked up the skin and began stripping it clean. With the last remaining flesh, she made a pile at her side. With the fat, she made another pile. Mre sat down beside Ruu and began sharpening her knife. When the edge felt sharp, she picked up a shank and cut the flesh from it in long, thin slices. The two women sat next to each other concentrating on their tasks.

As much to herself as to Mre, Ruu said, "It's going to be hard, very hard. We're going to have to be very frugal to make it. We need to work harder than we've ever worked before. The men have worked hard, but look at them now, they are weak and tired. It is us, the women, who must make the difference. The women are always the backbone. The women are the ones who must carry the Tribe. We must let nothing go to waste. Everything must be used. Every tiny bit of food is precious. A mouthful, one mouthful, could make the difference. We must make it through the winter. We must make it to spring. We must survive. Then, perhaps, there will be . . ."

"When was the last time you ate?" asked Mre. She stopped cutting. "When the stomach is empty, the mind runs like a panicked animal. Now is not the time to starve yourself. We cannot make it through the winter if we do not make it through the fall. We all need to stay well. Eat, Ruu. If we are to starve, let it be when we starve." Mre cut a piece of raw meat from the shank and handed it to Ruu.

Ruu stared at the meat in her hands. She put the meat in her mouth and held it there, then slowly chewed. She turned away from Mre as she swallowed it.

Mre cut all the meat from the shanks, then put the meat on the stones in the sun to dry. Ruu laid the pelt out flat on the logs with the fur side down. Mre picked up the water jug and poured water on the flesh side. Mre and Ruu washed it. Later, when they were in the Winter Cave, they would strip off the fur and soak the pelt in white oak bark to make it leather. For now, they rolled up the pelt, tied it, and put it in the storage hut.

Coming into the Hearthland from the far side near the woods, an old woman carried a full load of firewood in her arms. Only wisps of gray hair could be seen over the top of the wood.

Ruu ran over and said, "Mother, do you need help?"

"I'm fine." Rhae took a few more steps, stopped next to the hearth, and laid the wood down.

"Thank you," said Sra.

"There is no need to thank me for doing what must be done." Rhae said, smiling. She had a good smile and she smiled often as she walked about doing her chores, reminiscing to herself. A small, thin woman, bent now from her long years, her face had the wrinkles of one who had lived through the taut webs of time. She had seen and felt much, and now, her most heartfelt wish was to see the members of her "Family" grow old happily. She considered herself the mother of all the Tribe, not just her daughter Ruu and her son Krilu. But it was to the littlest children that she was most devoted. As grandmother to the children, she had found renewed purpose for her life. She danced with them, spun them around, slapped their behinds playfully. She sat with them, playing catch with a pinecone, laughing at their stories. The children loved her and she loved all the children, especially Jamu. She vowed that as long as she lived no child would grow uncared for. She took the responsibility of raising Jamu as naturally as everything else she did.

Rhae knelt beside the hearth. Leaning over, she blew gently on the glowing embers, then laid a few dried pine needles on them. The needles smoked, then glowed, then a small fire flickered. She quickly put shredded bark into the fire and blew again. The fire caught the bark. She put in two small pine twigs. Carefully, she built up the fire twig by twig, and then arranged the rocks around it into two circles, one inside the other.

Mre knelt over the low mound at the wall. The dirt felt warm in her hands as she pushed it away, uncovering a circle of rocks. She took a pair of sticks and rolled the rocks, as big as her hands, to Sra. Sra took a pair of sticks, picked up the rocks, and put them into the fire. Mre brushed away a layer of seared leaves. Under the leaves, bundles snuggled tightly together filled the shallow pit. Crinkled leaves covered each bundle. Mre picked up a bundle and unwrapped it. In the palm of her hand she held a freshly baked loaf of acorn bread, still soft and warm, black as coal, with the wrinkled imprint of the leaves and a small crescent moon drawn on its top. She nibbled it and nodded her approval as she handed it to Sra. Sra took a bite, nodded and smiled, then handed it back to her sister. The loaves of acorn bread, when cool, would be hard as rocks, look like fossils, and help keep the Tribe fed for the winter.

Mre brushed away another layer of leaves, then dug the rocks out of the bottom of the pit and rolled them over to Sra. Sra took her sticks and rolled the reheated rocks from the fire into the bottom of the pit. Mre covered the rocks in the pit with leaves and arranged the unbaked acorn loaves on top, then covered the bread with another layer of leaves. Sra encircled the leaves with another layer of hot rocks. The sisters filled the hole with dirt and patted it down into a low mound. The bread baked in this oven for twelve hours, and the women, baking continuously now, made two batches every day.

The fire burned and the work continued. Broda and Klena hung the antlers in the storage hut. Later, when the Tribe was in the Winter Cave, the antlers would be made into awls and needles. The men walked back to the logs and picked up the head of the elk. At the hearth, they laid the head down. The top of its skull had been cracked open and the head was almost completely stripped of flesh. They turned the head over, emptying it of the meat they had stripped off it. Broda cut away the jaw and laid it beside the hearth. He cut out the brain and laid it beside the jaw. The men picked up the head and walked out through the opening in the wall.

Rhae walked to the wall and brushed the leaves off its top. The well-worn stones felt cool and smooth under her hands, and made her smile. Many years ago, during the first summer when she, Klena, Broda, and the other children first lived here, they had built this stone wall. The wall protected them against prowling scavengers and kept the scents of the Tribe away from the animals that drank and fed at the stream. Rhae watched as Broda and Klena, hoping to attract an animal, any animal, tied the head of the elk to a tree stump in the meadow.

She watched Ruu walk back from the stream, through the

meadow, and through the opening in the wall. In each arm, Ruu carried a large clay pot filled with water. She laid both pots down beside the hearth.

Rhae knelt beside the hearth. She picked up a forked branch and took a hot rock from the inner circle nearest the fire. The rock hissed loudly when she dipped it into the first pot. Quickly, she dropped it into the second pot. Taking another rock from the fire, she cleaned it and dropped it into the second pot. She cleaned the jaw in the first pot, then dropped it into the second pot to cook. She added the meat scraps from the head to the cooking pot.

Ruu walked to the storage hut and returned carrying a stack of three wooden bowls. Dried blueberries filled the top bowl and a slab of dried deer meat covered it. In her other hand, she carried three thick shank bones. She sat down, picked up her knife, took the slab of meat, and began cutting it into small pieces. Mre walked to the storage hut and returned carrying a small clay pot. She took the pile of elk fat, put it into the clay pot, and placed the pot near the fire to melt it. Sra arranged a bed of clean leaves.

Steam rose from the cooking pot. Rhae took her forked stick, pulled the rocks out of the pot, and put them near the fire. She took hot rocks from the fire, cleaned them, and dropped them into the cooking pot. The water bubbled. She stood and walked to the woods.

Sitting around the fire, the three women each held a wooden bowl. In each bowl they put a handful of dried meat, a smaller handful of dried berries, then poured the melted fat over it. Using the shank bones, they pounded it all together until thick and mushy. They emptied the bowls on the bed of clean leaves and filled their bowls again.

"Have you seen Kru lately?" Sra asked Ruu.

"No. What's the matter with her now?"

"She will not tell me. She looks so weak and tired and her eyes look so empty, but I cannot find what is wrong with her. I listen to her breathing and it sounds well. I try roots, barks, teas, food. But nothing helps her."

"She still thinks of her mate too much," Mre said as she continued pounding her shank into her bowl. "It is hard to know when one has mourned too long, but he has been dead for more than a year. She should not mourn so long."

"He was my brother," said Ruu, "but he is dead. The Sickness is not new to us. We have seen it before. I, too, watched as my strong brother grew weaker and weaker, and the pain grew worse and worse, and his body felt as if on fire, and his mind wasted away until, mercifully, he died. All of us live under the curse of the Sickness. There is nothing any of us can do about it. But it's time for the living to help the living. How long will she hide in her hut? She's not sick, she's lazy."

Sra said quietly, "You should not talk like that, and so loud. Maybe she is sick."

"It's we who are sick!" shouted Ruu. "It's we who take care of her. We work from before dawn until late at night, while she lies in her hut and complains and eats. The empty bellies of the children groan in the night and our mates go hungry. She is fed while we are starving. We give her everything she wants. Why should she work? She rolls her eyes and complains, and we give her food. Why should she lift a hand to help any of us while we care for her? Her child is uncared for, while she cares only for herself. She does nothing but play with our hearts. If she is sick, let her die. If she is well, let her work. The lazy skunk!"

"Skunks are not lazy, my daughter," Rhae said calmly. Carrying a handful of dandelion greens, she walked toward the women. She cleaned the greens in the first pot, shredded the leaves, and dropped them into the bubbling water of the cooking pot. She knelt and stirred the water, looking into it as she said, "You have been listening to the children. That is what the children call her, even her son. Even her own son doubts that she is sick. She knows what is said about her. She knows, but it does not change her. I have tried everything I know to help her. I do not know what is wrong with her."

Rhae stopped, pulled the stick out of the pot and held it in her hands. "Kru is my youngest niece," she said as she raised her head. She looked at Sra, then at Mre, and said, "She is your sister." She turned her deep amber eyes to her daughter. "She is your cousin."

The women stopped working. Sra and Mre looked down at the ground, but Ruu looked up and stared at her mother. Rhae stared back, then turned away. "Her soul is her concern," Rhae said as she put the stick back into the cooking pot, "but her body is our responsibility." She stirred again.

Ruu pounded the shank down hard in her bowl.

CHAPTER 8

Rhae replaced the rocks in the cleaning and cooking pots. She picked up the intestines, stomachs, and throat of the elk from the logs and laid them beside the hearth. Gripping her hand tightly around the throat, she pulled it with her other hand. She pushed down on the stomachs, then gripping her hand tightly around the intestines, pulled with her other hand, squeezing the remaining wastes into the fire. Tilting the cleaning pot, she poured hot water through the throat, stomachs, and intestines. She put them into the cooking pot and stirred. She put her stick beside the hearth, stood, and walked to the woods.

From over the knoll, a girl walked toward the women, waving her right hand cheerfully. Her left hand held a dark brown walking stick, dirty at its bottom. She leaned against it as she walked through the village. Lashed to her back, bending her, she carried a heavy basket. Beside the hearth, she lowered the basket to the ground. It toppled over. Groundnuts rolled away. She turned and dove, fell on some, scampered back and forth, rolled and swept them into a pile, and finally, gathered them all back into the basket again.

Sra smiled and said, "You did well, Tya."

"Thank you, Mother."

"Your hands are muddy. Where did you go?"

She looked at her hands, then said, "I went to the little meadow on the other side of the pond. There are no more groundnuts left there. But there are still some beside Small Creek, where it joins Walking Stream. I'll go there before we leave."

Tya was the daughter of Sra and Mekla. She had light blond hair that hung down to her waist, smooth skin tinged with pink in her cheeks, and a quick, warm smile. With her head held high and a slight spring in her step, she walked like a young doe. She was a young woman at an in-between age. She felt too grown-up to be with the children, yet with the adults, she felt like a child. She felt bashful

about herself and was more comfortable when alone in the forest,
whistling at the birds, watching the animals, walking, and working.
Many days she walked through the forest, carrying her basket, filling
it with roots and nuts. All summer and autumn she had worked
hard, harder than she had ever worked before, gathering food for the
hungry Tribe. The hunger hurt, but if she could keep her mind off it,
and if she ate a little before she came home, she felt fine. She had
grown almost as skilled as Rhae or her mother in food-gathering.
When she finished her daily chores, she sat beside her aunt Mre to
learn craft skills. She wanted to learn everything. Tya wanted to
grow up quickly, but the other women thought she was growing into
a woman, and her obligations, quickly enough.

"I'll go wash the groundnuts." Tya lashed her basket tightly
around her waist, put her arms through the rawhide straps, and
lifted it. She groaned as the basket settled on her tired shoulders. The
women did not look up as Tya walked to the stream, but Sra smiled
proudly to herself.

While pounding the meat and berries, the women rocked rhythmi-
cally back and forth. In her bright, clear voice, Sra began singing a
simple melody, changing notes every time she brought the shank
down into the bowl. Mre joined in with her deep, smooth voice.
Together, their singing seemed to harmonize with the sounds of the
brisk autumn wind and the crisp leaves, tumbling down through the
slanting noonday sun.

Ruu emptied her bowl, then turned it over to fill it again. She
watched a dark red leaf fall into it. She stared at the dying leaf. The
chill in the air, even at noon, told her that the warm, soft days of
summer were gone and the hard realities of winter approached day
by day. She always seemed reminded of the hardness of their struggle
for life and the closeness of their deaths.

The tune of the women kept up the vigorous pace. Soon, they
would be burrowed in the Cave in Winter Valley. The singers raised
their voices higher. The tempo of their tune quickened.

Autumn is the season of impending change. This is the busy season. Work is hectic. Nerves are short. The tension of approaching
winter brings a final fury of vitality, while hope inspires, before
promise fades. There is much to do, so much work, and time, the
ever-moving sun, is unforgiving.

Sra cleaned off a flat rock near the hearth, then doused it with hot water from the cleaning pot. She pulled the intestines, stomachs, and throat out of the cooking pot and placed them on the rock.

Mre took a knife and cut the intestines into pieces as big as her hand, keeping the tube intact. Ruu cut the throat into similar pieces. After cutting the throat, she cut the stomachs into small pieces.

Sra pulled the jaw out of the cooking pot. She shaved off the long hair. Taking the strands of hair, she tied off one end of each piece of intestine, forming a pouch in each. She took the sweet berry and meat pemmican and stuffed the intestine pouches. After filling each pouch, she tied its other end.

Mre sliced the meat off the jaw. Ruu took the meat and chopped it into small pieces. She mixed it with the pieces of stomach.

Rhae returned carrying a basket of mustard greens, wild garlic, and green onions. She cleaned them, shredded the greens, peeled the garlic and onions, and put most of them into the cooking pot. She handed the rest to Ruu. Ruu chopped them well, then mixed them with the diced meat.

Sra tied off each piece of throat. She took the spicy meat, stuffed the throat pouches, and tied them. When the meat dried, the spicy sausages and sweet pemmican would help keep the Tribe fed for the winter.

Rhae put all the unused meat into the cooking pot, then stirred. She pulled the stick out and licked it. She smiled. The stew tasted good.

From over the knoll, a boy walked slowly toward the women. In his right hand, a leather sling dangled limply. His left hand held a dark brown spear, dirty at its bottom. His eyes moved constantly as he walked through the village. He looked disappointed as he tucked his sling beside the small leather pouch on his belt. He untied the sack lashed to his back. Sighing, he laid the empty sack down. "Nothing today," he said.

Mre said, "That is fine, Clata. You tried."

"I almost got a duck. Tomorrow, I will get something."

"Your hands are muddy. Where did you go?"

He looked at his hands, then shrugged his shoulders. He leaned over and sniffed the stew. "It smells good."

Clata was the son of Mre and Traro. He had light blond hair that hung down to his shoulders, slight beard hairs on his jaw, and a bold, earnest bearing. With his nimble feet, sharp reflexes, and keen eyes, he walked through the forest like a young buck. He was a clever boy, and a good hunter for his age. The men did not include him in their hunts and it hurt him to be treated like a child. He felt he was a hunter. He felt he was almost as good with his sling as Hsoro, and with his spear, he felt he was as good as anyone. Early in the summer, he single-handedly killed a fawn, a small one, with his spear. This winter he was going to make himself a fine bow and next year the men would have to include him in their hunts. Every day he practiced hard so he would be as good a hunter as his father and grandfather. Maybe better, he hoped. It was his weasel that hung in the shack. He stayed close to the village, killing small animals, and watching the women and children while the men were away. No one asked him to do it, but he felt, as a grown-up, that he must guard them. He took it upon himself with his usual seriousness. With his spear in one hand and his sling and pebble pouch on top of the stone wall, he would lean his chest against the inside of the wall and watch for every movement outside the village. The women could take care of the children and themselves, but they did not let Clata know. He wanted to feel grown-up, and the women did not want to hurt his feelings.

Clata leaned against the stone wall. He opened his pebble pouch, pulled out a groundnut, and ate it.

"Clata," Mre said, "go wash your hands. It's almost time to eat."

Clata climbed over the wall, ran across the meadow, and reached the stream just as Tya finished washing the groundnuts. He washed his hands quickly. Clata and Tya, smiling at each other, lifted the basket and carried it back to the village.

Sra came from the storage hut carrying the leather pouch that Mekla had filled with the kidneys, liver, and heart of the elk. She tilted the cleaning pot and poured hot water over them. She handed the kidneys to Mre. Mre cut them into small pieces. Ruu took the brain from beside the hearth, cleaned it, and cut it into pieces. Rhae put the kidneys and brain into the cooking pot.

Sra arranged two beds of clean leaves. Mre took the liver, cut it into pieces, and laid them on one of the beds. Ruu took the heart, cut it into pieces, and laid it on the other.

Tya and Clata returned with the basket of clean groundnuts. They looked through the basket, picked out the bigger ones, and put them into the fire.

CHAPTER 9

"Clata," Rhae said, "it is time to eat. Wake up the men."

He jumped to his feet and ran from hut to hut, hollering, stomping his feet in front of each hut, banging on the walls of one so hard that leaves fell off its roof.

Long moans from stretching bodies, and "Oh-huh," or "What do you want?" or "Stop! The roof is coming down!" came from the huts.

"Hurry! It's time to eat! Come on, Krilu, come on! It's time to eat, Mekla. Do not worry, Father, the roof will not come down. If it does, I'll fix it after we eat. Come on, Hsoro! Rhae says it's time to eat."

Clata clapped his hands and whistled loudly, making so much noise that the next time he passed in front of the hut of his father, a hand caught his ankle. Traro dove out and drove his shoulder into Clata, knocking him down. Clata rolled backward, somersaulted, landed on his feet, and rushed back at his father. He slammed his shoulder into Traro. Traro grabbed him as they both fell on the ground. They rolled in the dirt and leaves, first Traro on top, then Clata, then Traro. Growling and groaning, they wrestled each other until they both breathed hard. They tugged at each other slowly, then stopped. They held each other tightly as they lay on their sides. Traro let go of Clata, rolled on his back, smiled, then laughed. Clata rolled on his back and laughed, too. Traro stood up, offered his hand, helped his son up, and hugged him. He put his arm around Clata as they walked to the Hearthland.

"My son is strong," said Traro.

"Yes, he is strong," said Rhae, "but now he is dirty again. Both of you, go wash. It is time to eat. All of you," she shouted, "if you are hungry, wash!"

Traro and Clata jumped over the wall and raced to the stream. Traro won by a stride. Mekla awoke dazed, as usual, but still managed a small grin as he walked by the women. Krilu pushed his hands through his hair, pulling out the tangles, then yawned, stretching his arms and expanding his bare chest. Hsoro looked tired, worn, and pale, the same as when he went to sleep. He walked to the stream, alone, shivering with his arms across his stomach.

"Come on, children, come on. No more games. It is time to eat," Rhae said, slapping at their behinds as she gathered the children. They ran around and away from her, covering their behinds. Rhae smiled until she saw only four children. "Where is Jamu?" she asked.

"We were playing hide and seek," answered the oldest girl, "but we could not find him."

"Jamu!" Rhae shouted, "the game is over. Come home! Jamu, where are you?"

She looked around the woods. Her face grew worried. She listened and, from behind the stone wall at the pine tree, heard giggling. She snuck to the wall and leaned over it. On the other side, hid Jamu. His small hands, trying to muffle his laughing, covered his freckled face.

"Come on, you rascal." She helped him up the wall. From the top, he jumped into her arms. She spun him around, his feet flying. The other children laughed and clapped their hands.

She let him down, then petted his sandy-colored hair. "Come on, children, it is time to eat. Wash your hands well."

The children raced to the stream.

"Use the sand from the bottom," she shouted after them, "and scrub hard to try to clean the walnut stains off your hands."

Rhae looked at her hands. They felt a bit stiff in the mornings and a persistent pain ran through them in the evenings. The stains from gathering the black walnuts made her hands look leathery. In the fall, she gathered walnuts and they always stained her hands. She rubbed her hands together. They were still brown. After so many years, she knew that the stains would be gone by spring. She hoped her hands would hurt less.

The women returned from their huts carrying wooden bowls. The men returned from the stream carrying thin willow sticks. Rhae put four rocks into the fire. The men cleaned up around the hearth, stacking the larger twigs around the fire and throwing the smaller twigs and dead leaves into it. The fire flared up brightly just as the children returned from the stream. They ran around the fire, extending their clean, but still stained, hands for all to see.

Sra put a piece of liver into each bowl and Mre passed the bowls around. Rhae walked to the children, took the meat out of their bowls, and laid each piece on top of the inside circle of hot rocks. The adults stuck the pointed ends of their sticks through the meat. They dug the other ends into the ground against the bottom of the outside circle of rocks. Their sticks leaned against the top of the inside circle of rocks and the meat drooped over the fire. Rhae laid a piece of meat on a rock for Kru. She stuck the point of a stick through a piece of meat, walked to the far side of the fire, and pushed the end of the stick into the ground.

The sound of slowly rustling leaves reached the Tribe. Everyone stopped and looked in the same direction. Wrapped in a thick bear-skin hide, Jascha shuffled slowly toward them. Wheezing softly, he stopped every few steps and rested against his gnarled oaken cane. Rhae stood up and walked to his side. He put his hand on top of her arm and leaned against her. They walked to a boulder beside the hearth. She helped him down. He sighed softly, then leaned forward until his hands rested on top of his cane and his chin rested on the back of his hands.

Near the opening in the wall, Krilu lay on his stomach, staring at the cooking meat. Broda, his crutch leaning against the wall, sat on the ground with his back against the wall. With one knee on the ground and an elbow on his other knee, Traro knelt near the fire. Hsoro sat beside him. Mekla sat next to Klena. Beside Klena, Jascha leaned close to the fire. A streak of afternoon sunlight fell through the oak tree and across his face, brightening his scraggly chin whiskers and withered mouth, while shadows covered his half-closed eyes and bald head. Sra sat on the ground beside him, watching the meat cooking over the fire. On the other side of the bed of leaves with the pieces of heart on it, Mre knelt and put the stack of twigs and an oak branch into the fire. Ruu sat near the fire, stirring the stew. Tya sat with her legs tucked under her and often looked toward the women, hoping they would ask for her help, and once she glanced at Clata. Like his father, Clata knelt on one knee while leaning on his other. Between Tya and Clata, the five children, shuffling from foot to foot, elbowing each other, moved impatiently closer to the fire as Rhae turned their meat over on the rocks.

Sra brought a wooden grill from the storage hut. Taking the water jug, she poured water over the grill. She put the grill on the four large rocks. She moved it once, then took her hands away slowly.

The grill stayed. The fire hissed as the water drops danced on the grill until they shrank smaller and smaller, then disappeared. Sra laid the pieces of heart on the grill. The heart crackled from the heat. A drop of fat fell and a tiny flame burst, followed by an enlarging, fading circle of smoke. Everyone watched eagerly as the meat cooked over the fire. Sra took a forked stick and turned over the pieces of heart. They were golden brown, the skin bubbling and popping, the blood dripping from it. One by one, they pulled their sticks away from the fire and put the liver into their bowls, except Krilu who blew hard on his piece of smoking hot liver, then bit into it. Sra pulled off the piece of liver for Jascha and put it into his bowl. She laid the first piece of heart into it and handed the bowl to Jascha.

Jascha leaned his cane against his thigh and took the bowl, cradling it in the palms of his hands. He lifted the bowl to his nose, sniffed, raised his eyebrows, and exhaled, nodding his head. He picked up the piece of heart, blew on it, and put it into his mouth. He chewed and chewed while the Tribe waited and waited. With a loud gulp, he swallowed. A grin, a small toothless grin, grew on his face. Jascha patted his skinny stomach and the Tribe laughed loudly.

Quickly, everyone handed their bowls to Sra and she hurried to fill them. Rhae, still laughing, filled the bowls of the excited children. Sniffs and snorts, stomach-patting, and pleasant laughter filled the village.

CHAPTER 10

"Where is my food?" The raspy voice of Kru cut through the cheerful Tribe.

The contented face of Jascha turned pale, the sides of his mouth drooped. Ruu turned toward the hut, clenched her fists, and pounded hard on her thighs. Jamu stood, took a step toward the hut, then sat back down and stared at the ground. Hsoro stared at the ground, too. Everyone stopped eating.

"Where is my food?"

Rhae said, "It is coming."

"I am hungry now!" Kru shouted.

"We are all hungry," Rhae said as she filled a bowl with meat. She walked to the hut, knelt in front of it, and laid the bowl inside.

"Is that all?" Kru demanded.

Rhae took a deep breath, then answered, "Yes, that is all."

"You are starving me! The men killed a whole elk and this is all you are giving me?"

"Yes. It is not much but it is the same as all of us. That is all we can have or we will not make it through the winter."

"But I am hungry now!"

"Then eat what is given you and be satisfied. That is all there is."

"But it is not nearly enough."

"But it is all we can have." Rhae looked tired as she stood up slowly. She took a few steps, then turned and looked back at the hut, shaking her head sadly. With a frown on her face and her head down, she walked back to the Hearthland.

Putting his bowl on the ground with the meat uneaten, Jascha walked away. He shuffled slowly through the fallen leaves, leaning on his cane. Rhae ran after him. He heard her coming and stopped. Without turning around, he lifted up his cane and waved it from side to side. She came no closer. She watched him walk stiffly back to his

hut, bend down, and crawl inside. Staring helplessly at his hut, she
turned around and saw everyone staring.

The Tribe picked at the food apathetically. First Hsoro, then the
others, passed the barely eaten food to the children who quickly and
quietly ate it. The groundnuts burned in the fire.

Krilu picked up his bowl and handed it to Ruu. She dipped it into
the stew and handed it back. Ruu dipped her own bowl into the stew.
One by one, everyone held out their bowls for stew. Ruu filled each
bowl, while Sra passed around loaves of acorn bread. Quickly and
quietly, they ate the stew. They dipped the bread in and ate it. They
turned their bowls over into gaping mouths, then handed their empty
bowls back to Ruu. Grateful smiles greeted her as she filled each
bowl with a small second helping. They ate all the stew. They
cleaned their bowls with the bread and ate all of it, too.

They put their bowls down. Some lay on their backs with their
hands behind their heads and looked into the sky, while others stood
up, walked around, shaking their legs and stretching, then sat down
again.

Krilu lay on his stomach with a blade of grass hanging from his
mouth. He asked, "Do we hunt tonight?"

Hsoro and Traro nodded their heads.

"Do we go hunt beyond Far Mountain again?"

Hsoro shook his head and Traro answered, "No."

Krilu raised his head and his voice, "Why not? There are more
elks there. I say we go back and get a fat female."

"No," Traro said, "they have gone away. It is too far. We must
find something closer." His face looked tired, his eyes sad, as he
shook his head and quietly said, "The forest is bare of game. They
have all run away. They are scared. Where have so many gone?
What have we done wrong?"

Krilu asked loudly, "Where do we go?"

Traro shook his head. His chin sunk to his chest. He sat in silence
while the Tribe waited.

"Where do we go?"

"Up Broad Mountain." All eyes turned to Hsoro. His head hung
down and shadows covered his face, but his quiet voice carried
clearly, "We go to Stone Meadow."

"Why there?" Krilu demanded.

Hsoro raised his head slowly and stared at Krilu. Krilu stared back defiantly. Hsoro raised his eyes to the sky. "It will be clear tonight, and cold, the coldest night yet. The animals will be hungry, the meadow has food, and we will be waiting."

"I want to go there this afternoon," said Rhae, "and take the children with me."

Hsoro smiled slightly. "Leave food for the animals. Do not strip the meadow."

"We will leave enough food, and stay downwind."

He nodded his head.

"I wish you well," said Rhae.

"I wish us all well."

Grunts of agreement echoed among the Tribe. Everyone, down to the youngest child, knew exactly how much food there was. No one hid the truth. Tonight would be cold, tomorrow colder, and the food supply would not stock itself. The women gathered better than they expected this year. The animals, their usual competition, were scarce. Not even Broda, the old hunter, could ever remember so few animals and the hunting so bad. But the men, born and raised in this forest, were good hunters. Hsoro was a fine stalker who could track any animal. As for Traro, no one doubted his extraordinary hunting skills. Yet this year, filled mostly with disappointments and frustrations, the hunters often, too often, returned to their hungry families downhearted and empty-handed. It hurt them, but they knew they must not fail. They knew, every time they saw the wide, sad eyes of the children and their swollen bellies.

Hsoro spoke softly, without raising his head, "We will sleep now, and leave after dusk."

As Klena stood up he said, "Tomorrow night is the Ceremony. It begins at sunset. Be home early."

Klena helped Broda up. The two old men leaned against the stone wall and looked out over the meadow. Clata stood beside them. One of the boys touched Jamu and said, "It!" and the children raced into the woods with Jamu running after them. Sra, Mre, and Ruu picked up the eating bowls and walked to the stream to wash them. Tya brought two wide baskets from the storage hut and helped Rhae fill one with pemmican and the other with sausages. They each carried a basket back to the storage hut. The men stood up slowly and straggled back to their huts to sleep.

CHAPTER 11

The huts of the Tribe were conglomerations of rocks, wood, and bark. Rubble was often all that was left of them when the Tribe returned in the spring. The rocks around the outside and the pine poles pounded into the ground remained, and sometimes, the frames of straight birch poles lashed to the pine poles with vines. During the winter, hungry animals stripped away the walls of birch bark. The weight of the winter snows collapsed the roofs of birch and pine branches. Each spring, the Tribe rebuilt their huts.

The doorway of each hut faced the Hearthland. A door of lashed birch branches leaned against the side of each hut. Every hut was built low; the small doorway forced stooping, or crawling on hands and knees, to enter. Even the shortest adults had to slouch when inside. After removing the sharp rocks, the ground inside was trampled flat, then covered with pine needles. Over the needles were deerskin hide blankets. Often on the ground next to them were a few unusually shaped or colored stones, crystal or rose quartz, or a contorted pinecone, a curious-looking twig, or pretty flowers. A leather pouch for keeping the trinkets lay with them. Beside them lay a small pouch of carefully chosen pebbles with a leather sling tied around it. In the corner by the doorway stood a long bow and a leather quiver filled with arrows. A stack of wooden bowls sat in the other corner. A spear leaned against the outside.

The Tribe owned few things. Everything they owned, they had to carry, and it added more weight along with their food and clothes. All that they needed had to come from the forest. When it was time to move, everything they did not need in the Cave, they left.

Carrying their fishing poles, Broda and Klena walked through the village. Clata joined them, carrying his. They walked over the knoll, disappearing step by step until the backs of their heads slid beneath the top of the knoll and only the tops of the fishing poles could be seen gliding toward Teardrop Pond.

The women gathered around the hearth. They squatted beside the fire, rubbing their hands over the coals.

"I'd like to gather Arrowheads from the far side of the pond," said Sra.

Mre said, "It's going to be cold rooting on the bottom of the pond, trying to pull them up with our toes, and if they float away, we have nothing to show for all our work."

"But they taste so good," said Sra. "Maybe we can find a sunny place where the water isn't too cold."

"I would like to get some Cattails, too," said Mre. "We can grind them into flour and I could use the stalks for making baskets."

"Maybe we can catch a turtle or two before they bury themselves in the mud," added Sra. "Winter is coming too soon this year. Soon we will not be able to get any."

"Can I go with you?" asked Tya.

"I'd like that," said Sra.

"I will go with you, too," said Ruu.

"Go without her," said Rhae, "she will come later." Taking Ruu by the hand, Rhae walked to her hut.

Everyone in the Tribe over the age of five wore a True Knot. At the age of five, parents took their child to a secluded place for a simple ceremony. The mother and father tied a knot in the middle of a plain strip of leather, then each took hold of an end, and pulled. Together, they said to the child, "This is your True Knot. Use it when you must speak the truth. Use it when the truth is hard to say." The parents tied the strip of leather around the neck of the child. The True Knot was one of the most precious possessions of the Tribe. They wore it for life.

Rhae crawled into her hut with Ruu following her. She sat down and Ruu sat across from her. She bowed her head and took off her True Knot. She laid it gently into the hands of Ruu.

"My daughter," Rhae said softly, "your bones show through your skin. In the last week, I have seen you stumble three times. Enough of this. If you do not rest, you will make yourself sick."

"This is no time to rest."

"This is no time to make yourself sick. This is a hard life, but you are a woman and you have your responsibilities. You must take care of yourself. You are carrying a child. When will you tell him, Ruu?"

"Not so loud, Mother. I will tell him when we are in the Winter

Cave, not before. Hsoro has enough problems without knowing this. I will continue to work. I must. We must have enough food until spring. By then, I may be unable to work."

"You must take better care of yourself this time."

"I wish I was not carrying. There is more important work for me. The Tribe cannot feed another without me working. When we are in the Cave, I will take better care."

"You will."

"This will be better than the last time. I did what I must. My hands did not shake. My heart remained still. She was weak. Before she knew of herself, I sent her back. I could do it again."

"This time you will both be fine."

"—if there is food for us."

"There will be food in your breasts if you take care of yourself."

"I will take better care of myself," Ruu smiled and said, "and next spring, you will be a grandmother."

"Good," said Rhae, smiling back.

Ruu bowed her head and took off her True Knot. She laid it gently into the hands of Rhae.

"I am worried. Hsoro looks terrible. He barely eats. He sleeps little. He rarely speaks, even to me. His eyes look far away. He buries himself in his problems. He blames himself. He questions himself. He is sure there is something he could do, but he does not know what. He is in pain and I do not know how to help him."

Rhae moved closer to her and said, "You can help him with your love. That is what he needs. That is what fills him. When he is full of his problems, he will speak. Listen to him with an open heart. Speak truly to him. Hsoro is a good and smart man. You have chosen a warm, gentle mate. We have chosen an honest, caring leader. He has done all he can. In my heart, I am sure, he will do all he must."

Each holding the True Knot of the other, the two women, mother and daughter, sat in silence.

CHAPTER 12

The afternoon sunlight bounced down through the leaves and broke into patches on the ground. The trunks of the aspen and birch trees glowed as if filled with a light of their own. The oak tree covered its broad trunk with its own shadow. At its roots, a gray squirrel stopped and searched. It picked up an acorn, jumped onto the top of the stone wall, scampered over, and disappeared beyond the knoll. Outside the wall, a stubborn worm and a determined robin struggled until the robin pulled the worm from the ground and flew away. In the sunny meadow, a crow, in all its intense blackness, sat contentedly on the head of the elk and picked at its blank, brown eyes. Startled, it flew quickly away.

"Children, it is time to go. Come along, now. Do not forget your baskets. Come along, children," Rhae called as she walked through the village. The children raced back from the woods. They helped each other tie their baskets on their backs. They tied leather pouches to their waists. Rhae tied a basket on her back, a leather pouch to her waist, and began walking.

Five children followed Rhae as she walked on a leaf-covered path through the woods. On the far side of the woods, the path curled up the slope of Broad Mountain, down into a narrow ravine, and across the almost dry bed of Small Creek. Up, down, and across, then up, down, and across, they followed the path as it twisted up the mountain.

The forest shimmered with life. The treetops sparkled in the cool sunlight. Lying dormant under the thick green of summer, autumn had turned countless leaves into countless colors. A sharp gust shook the branches and a shower of leaves fell, pattering the dark ground. Twirling maple seeds spun to the earth. The air smelled heavy with life and death. Two chipmunks, their claws scratching loudly, ran after each other around and around the trunk of a maple tree. Up the tree, across its bobbing branches, and down again they ran. An abandoned nest tumbled from a bare tree. It rolled down the ravine and stopped on a clump of gray moss. Dancing in and out of spaces between the baring branches, the sun winked at the tiny band of food gatherers. Dwarfed by the size and splendor of the forest, by its extravagant bounty and callous indifference, the small group roamed on.

Rising from the ravine, the path turned nearly back on itself as it bent around large, granite boulders. Back and forth, and up, farther up, the path climbed. Rhae knelt, picked up a stiff branch, and broke the dead twigs off it. Leaning on it, she continued up. Her moccasined feet made barely a sound. A rabbit stopped suddenly at the edge of the path. Rhae stopped and the children stopped behind her. The rabbit ran ahead on the path and five small brown bunnies followed her. The rabbit hopped under some bushes, stopped and waited for her children, then disappeared into a thicket. Rhae, with the children following her, walked to the thicket.

Rhae stopped, spread her arms out wide, and said, "This is Sassafras. It grows in dense thickets like this. Everyone of these small bushes is Sassafras. Sniff near the roots, children. It smells sweet. Jamu, let me see your hand. Open your hand out flat and put all your fingers together. It looks oval like one of its leaves. Now, stick out your thumb. Your hand looks like another of its leaves. If you had two thumbs on both sides of your hand, it would look like another of its leaves. Do you see all three kinds of leaves on these plants? Good. This is going to take some work. A boy and a girl work together. Jamu, you and I will work together. Find a small bush with a thin, green stem. Grab it near the roots. Are you ready? One-two-three-PULL! Try pulling it from side to side. Pull harder! We did it, Jamu. This is a long root. Did you get one out yet, children? Good. Shake the dirt off the root, break off the stem, and put the root into your basket. Take a leaf from the plant and chew it. It tastes good and spicy. Take a few leaves, we will dry them. Powdered, they are good for thickening stews. Come along, we must keep going. We can come back for more. Do you remember Sassafras Tea? It is good when the weather is cold. This winter I will show you how to make it. Just heat some water, drop in a handful of clean roots, and wait until the water turns red, and your nose tickles, and you cannot wait any longer, then it is done. It is good for you, too. It lowers fevers and is good for your stomach. Best of all, it tastes wonderful."

The path climbed and the trees thinned. After a sharp turn, the path leveled off and the trees stopped. The sun hovered over the treetops to the west. Rhae and the children stopped at the sunny eastern side of Stone Meadow. Scattered in the meadow were white, but discolored, stones. Most were leaning over or fallen down. Shaped into squares or crosses, the few stones still standing upright cast long, odd shadows. Faded after years of erosion was the writing carved into the stones. No one understood the words and numbers. Sunflowers grew around the stones in the meadow.

"Sunflowers," Rhae said. "Look at them. They look like suns growing from the earth. Sometimes, I feel that they grow so big just to show off. When I was a young girl, I loved running through meadows of Sunflowers. They are old now, a little faded, their soft petals wrinkled by age. They are past the peak of their beauty, but they are still useful. This will take some stretching. Bend the top of the plant down and pull off the old flowers. Find a dried one but not so dry that the seeds have fallen off. The seeds are small but good to eat raw, and delicious roasted. They are good for you, so gather as much as you want. We get oil from these seeds by crushing then boiling them. When the oil rises to the top, we take the rocks from the pot, let it cool, and skim the oil off the water. We need these old flowers, yet I wish that Sunflowers could stay young forever.

"This is not a Bird's Nest," she said. "See, it is the top of this plant. Before they dried up, these flowers were white, broad, and big, like big snowflakes. Do you remember them? You can call them Bird's Nests, but do not forget to look down to the ground. Grab the bottom of the plant and pull hard. Do not jerk, its roots are deep. Yes, the roots are long and woody. We call these plants Wild Carrots. We will wash the roots and eat them soon, or dry and grind them into a powder to make a good warming drink.

"Do you remember Dandelions? These are the plants with the low, spiky leaves. We picked and ate the young leaves in the spring. Later, the Dandelions bloomed with bright yellow flowers, but by then, the leaves were too bitter to eat. Do you remember the fuzzy balls of white seeds that you blew off in the summer and watched float away on the warm breeze? Now, you remember. Good. They are old and wrinkled now, but underneath they are as good as ever. Pull them up gently. Try to get as much of the root as possible. Shake it off well and put it in your basket. We will roast these roots

until their insides are dark brown, then grind them into powder. It
will make a good hot drink to keep us warm and healthy through the
winter.

"See this plant? It looks like a Dandelion, but feel its stem. It is
stiffer and the plant is taller, nearly as tall as you, Jamu. If you look
closely, you can see a few blue ragged flowers. The flowers fold up in
the afternoon, but they are still pretty. These plants are called Chicory and they bloom in the late summer and autumn. It is too late to
eat the leaves. We have to find them in the early spring soon after the
ground thaws. But, the roots are still good. Pull this one up just like
a Dandelion. Be careful, do not pull too hard, we need as much of
the root as possible. We roast Chicory, too, and it makes a good hot
drink that settles your stomach.

"See the leaf on this plant? It looks like the webbed foot of a goose.
We call this plant Goosefoot, or Wild Spinach. Here is another way
to learn this plant. Its leaves are pale green and look dusty, as if there
is a fine white powder on them. Underneath, its leaves look whiter
and more dusty. If you put a drop of water on the leaf, the water
would run off and the leaf would stay dry, or the water would sit on
it without getting the leaf wet. Of course, when we boil them, they
get wet. There is Wild Spinach until the frost comes. Find the youngest, smallest, tenderest plants, pull them up whole, and put them in
your basket. When you find a tall plant, pick its topmost leaves, they
taste best. Do not take any old leaves, they are too bitter. On the tall
plants, you will find a dense cluster of seeds still in their husks.
Carefully, put them in your pouch. We will sort them at home. The
seeds are tiny, hard, and brownish black. We could come back later
for them, but take them now. We need them. We use the seeds for
cereal, or grind them into a powder to add to acorn flour.

"Come with me to the edge of the meadow. We have found some
fruit. Get down on your hands and knees. I doubt you can get any
dirtier than you already are. These are rare, but easy to remember.
Do you see the thin, straw-colored husks? Inside each husk is one,
smooth, yellow-green berry. These are good. The ones with the husks
still closed can be kept a full moon or two, and grow sweeter without
being on the plant. We can eat sweet Ground Cherries without coming back. Try some that are open. Good?

"This should be easy for you. Do you know what these dark blue
berries are? Yes, they are Blueberries. Let us sit awhile. We are al-

most done. Rest, you have worked hard today. Eat as many berries as you want. They are good fresh, but we will dry most of them this year so they will keep.

"Are you full yet? Good. Pick more berries. Take as many as you can. Fill your baskets. Quickly, dusk is coming. I want us home before it is dark. All done? Good. Be sure your baskets are tied on tightly. Do not forget your pouches. Does everyone have a pouch? Good. Come along."

CHAPTER 13

From Stone Meadow, they heard a solitary cricket. A flock of large, black grackles settled into the meadow. Their iridescent heads bobbed relentlessly up and down as they picked the meadow clean of insects. The soothing sound of the cricket stopped. A circling hawk swooped down and soared up with a struggling squirrel in its claws. At the edge of the meadow, in an upper branch of a maple tree, an owl slept and waited for darkness. Underneath, on the ground, a chipmunk filled one side of her mouth with seeds, then the other, scampered into the bushes, and disappeared, her winter stock fuller.

With their backs bent by their heavy baskets, Rhae and the children walked happily down the path toward home. The path turned down steeply and the children began walking faster and faster. The two brothers started to race. The children began laughing and running and scurrying down the mountain. They jumped over protruding rocks and fallen trees. They ran through narrow curves of worn granite. One of the girls lost her balance and bumped Jamu. Jamu stumbled. He grabbed Rhae. She dropped her stick and grabbed the trunk of a tree. They spun around it once together, then Jamu lost his grip. He staggered a few steps, then fell. Rhae, her basket dangling from her shoulders, dropped to the ground. The children slowed, bumping into each other, then sat down. They untied their baskets, slipped them off, and rested. Jamu gathered the dumped roots and berries back into his basket, while Rhae smiled.

From the other side of the ravine, they heard a loud rustling of leaves. A few pebbles slid down the slope. Into a small clearing, lumbered a big, brown bear followed by two pudgy cubs. The bear stopped. She sniffed the ground, then raised her head and looked around. Her dark brown eyes searched for any movement. She reared back on her hind legs, stretched to her full height, and backed into a rough-barked birch tree. With her head cocked and her paws swinging in front of her, she rubbed her back against the tree, groan-

ing contentedly to herself. The tree trembled from her weight and a
flurry of bright yellow leaves fluttered down around her. The two
cubs scuffled, playfully swatting at the falling leaves. One of them
missed and slapped the other on its nose. Growling, they grabbed
each other, wrestling and rolling on the ground, kicking dirt over the
edge and down into the ravine. The mother bear walked away from
the small clearing. Her cubs stopped fighting and quickly followed
her.

The children covered their faces and laughed into their hands, but
Rhae stared at the small clearing.

She stood and hurried down the ravine. Grabbing handfuls of dirt
and roots, she climbed the other side. She slipped, slid partway
down, scratching her stomach, and started up again. Rhae pulled
herself up into the clearing.

At the edge of the clearing, brightened by the last, faint rays of
sunlight, stood a tall plant. Walking nearer, Rhae saw again the pale
yellow tassels at its top. The stalk underneath it looked exhausted,
gnarled by age, already faded and dead along the edges. Two long,
green leaves, withered brown at the ends, clung to opposite sides of
the stalk. She walked around the plant, staring at it. She stopped and
stood next to it. They were the same height. Next to her heart, one
growth, one last feeble growth survived. A dry, frail husk, partly
shredded, hung down from it. Strands of dim gold threads protruded
from inside it. Small, irregular, dry seeds lined the growth in ragged
rows. Some of the seeds were dark yellow, some were red, others
black, most were gone. Rhae took the growth from the stalk and
knelt. She thought back many years to her youth. Tears filled her
eyes. A tear slid down her cheek and onto the husk. Rhae raised her
eyes toward the sky and softly said, "Corn."

Rhae rose slowly. She tucked her discovery inside her hide, then
climbed down the ravine, and up to the children. The curious children gathered around her. She smiled but said nothing. Lifting her
basket, tying it around her waist, then picking up her stick, she
walked down the path. She held the corn firmly in her other hand.
The children tied on their baskets and followed quickly.

From high in the forest, a wood thrush sang. It started its rich, low
melody, then stopped, tried again, paused, then broke into clear, full-
throated song. Its flute-like melody accompanied the setting sun. A
pair of bats winged fitfully, batting insects into their mouths. A

mourning dove cooed. A cold wind whined through the trees. The heavy branches creaked and groaned. Dying leaves pattered the darkening ground. Dusk, that dim afterglow, that unearthly gray light that seems to come from everywhere, yet nowhere, crept into the forest.

The ravine widened. The path dipped into it and leveled off at the bottom of the mountain. Jamu, hungry and wobbly, too tired to go on, stumbled, grabbed a tree, and leaned against it. Rhae motioned for the other children to stop. They took off their baskets and sat down. Rhae stopped and took off her basket. She sat against a tree, put her stick down, closed her eyes, and listened contentedly to the peaceful sounds around her. One particular sound caught her attention. With a broad smile brightening her face, she reached out to Jamu. They walked off hand in hand.

"Listen," she whispered. They both heard the hollow, muffled drumming of a grouse. The leaves crackled underfoot as they walked. They heard it again, and tiptoed closer. They saw a shadowy brown grouse dug into its nest, camouflaged under a tangle of vines. Its wings began to whir. A sharp crack broke the calm air. Rhae shook violently. The grouse shot up and away. Rhae grabbed her chest, screamed, slumped to her knees, and fell forward.

"Grandmother?" Jamu asked. He watched her back rise, fall, then stop. He knelt beside her and shook her. She did not move.

"Grandmother?"

CHAPTER 14

Every head in the village turned simultaneously. Traro grabbed his bow and quiver and ran from his hut. Carrying his sling and pebble pouch, Hsoro ran from his. Their bare feet slapped on the ground as they sprinted together. The rest of the Tribe raced to keep up with them. Traro arrived first and stood over Rhae. Hsoro stopped beside her. His sling fell from his hand. He dropped to his knees and gently rolled her over. Her empty eyes stared up at him. Blood gathered on her chest, trickled down her side, and onto his feet. Hsoro lowered his head to her chest. He leaned his ear against it. He heard nothing. The children, huddling together, covered their faces and cried. The rest of the Tribe gathered around her as Hsoro stroked her face. He closed her eyelids. He slid his arms under her and picked her up. She hung limply in his arms. Ruu held her mother's hand. The other hand dangled. The circle parted. Hsoro carried Rhae home.

"What has happened?" shouted Kru from her hut.

"Rhae is dead," said Sra.

If Kru said anything, no one heard her. No one else spoke.

Hsoro carried Rhae through the village, over the knoll, and down to Teardrop Pond. The rest of the Tribe stayed in the village. Only Klena, a few steps behind, followed.

The twilight faded, a fresh chill settled in the air, and to the west, a single star glimmered above the treetops. Hsoro laid her down beside the pond. He looked at her, and then, with a silent nod, walked away.

Klena looked at Rhae. He remembered a brash little girl who had come here and grown up with him; a lively young woman who often came to him to talk, to laugh, and sometimes, to cry; the lovely mate of his brother, so happy, so cheerful, and so nervous; a strong woman who gave birth to three children, and buried one, and buried her mate; a brave woman who strangled the rattlesnake that bit Broda; an old woman, confident in herself and unselfish in her devotion to the Tribe, loving and caring for all of them; and above all, a dear friend. Now, she lay dead.

He knelt beside her and said, "So many times I wanted to thank you for being alive, for just being alive with me, but I kept putting it off and putting it off for another time." He laid his hand on her cheek. "Now, we have no more time together. Yet, still, I have never said it. I do not know if you can hear me, but now, I will say it." His voice trembled, "Thank you, Rhae."

His hands shook as he undressed her. Her bones showed through her skin. She looked so pale, so frail. He stared at her. His eyes fixed on the hole in her chest. His hands reached up and felt for a hole in his own.

He lifted her in his arms and waded into Teardrop Pond. He cleaned her wound, bathing her as if she was a baby. Unbraiding her hair, he let it flow freely around her shoulders. He washed her face, caressing it and smoothing the ends of her mouth so she would be forever smiling. Cradling her in his arms, he softly hummed a lullabye she often sang to the children. She floated lightly, gently bobbing on the small, passing waves. He lifted her out of the water and walked to shore. He kissed her on the forehead as the last drops of water trickled down. He held her for a moment, one last moment for the two old friends to be alone together. "What is most cruel about death," Klena whispered, "is that we always want one more moment together, and we can never have it." He hugged her to him. "Death always comes too soon." Tears trickled down his cheeks.

Hsoro and Traro gathered armfuls of pine boughs. They handed them to Mekla, who silently, carefully built a funeral bier. With his own hands, in his own world, he prepared it for another world, a world without time. Respect filled his every move. Four stout branches he tied securely with leather. With vines, he fastened the boughs. He smoothed the bier with his hands. When he finished, he examined it, not to judge its perfection, but to judge the purity of his own heart. The shaman-to-be motioned to Hsoro and Traro. They lifted it and carried it to the shore of the pond.

Klena laid Rhae down on her funeral bier.

Hsoro and Traro carried her back to the village. They laid her in front of her hut, then the Tribe formed a circle.

Klena took an oak branch. He put the end of it into the hearth. When the branch caught fire, he carried it to the empty hut of Rhae.

He circled the hut, lighting each corner of it as he chanted, "All our lives are fleeting. We must say good-bye. Earth and sky are everlasting. We all must die." He threw the burning branch on the hut.

The dry wood burst into flames. Wild shadows danced behind the Tribe, standing still and silent. The flames quickly stretched toward the sky, then, almost as quickly, the hut crumbled to the earth. Thick smoke rose from the hut. Glowing ashes fell from the wood. The fire quietly burned down. The brightness darkened.

The hooting of a lone owl called from the heart of the woods. Partly hidden behind the treetops and the clouds, the pale moon looked down. A cold wind shook the trees. Leaves fell into the stream. They whirled and spun until they disappeared or sank. Walking Stream turned away, then back, its tone deeper.

Beside the stream, a silent procession walked along a path. Klena led them. He held a drum and, with the palm of his hand, thumped it in a slow, heartbeat rhythm. A few steps behind walked Ruu, carrying the wooden bowl of her mother and, in it, the small pouch containing her possessions. Next followed the men, each shouldering a corner of the bier. In a single line walked the children, carrying the bowls of the Tribe. The women carried empty baskets. Broda, hobbling last at his own pace, ended the procession. Jascha could not come, and Kru would not.

Silhouetted by the moon, two beech trees stood tall. Their branches joined with each other, the moonlight, and their shadows. Dark leaves, already touched by the cold, filled the trees. A pair of thick trunks led down to sprawling roots. Together they had grown, and still together, the old trees arched over the entrance to the Grove.

The procession waded across the stream. It washed over their legs. They climbed up the other shore. At the top, they gathered again. They walked on the path between the two trees.

The trees in the Grove grew in neat, orderly rows. From the entrance at the north, they formed straight rows from east to west. The densely branched trees with wide crowns stood almost bare, stripped of their leaves by the passing autumn and of their fruit by the foraging Tribe. A few of the bright red fruits, looking black in the night, still drooped from the tallest, oldest trees. The trees were younger and smaller as the procession walked south across the Grove. They laid Rhae near a sapling.

The men knelt. They took sharp, strong sticks and started digging. After breaking through the hard surface, they put down the sticks and dug with their bare hands. The sound of thrown dirt, swishing through the air and falling to the ground, filled the silence between the drumbeats.

In the shadows at the edge of the Grove, Klena sat alone, rocking back and forth, humming quietly to himself. The penetrating power of the heartbeat rhythm rippled through the air and rumbled through the ground.

Unconsciously, the Tribe breathed as one. The women and children knelt beside Rhae. Ruu held Rhae's head in her lap. Sra and Mre sat on either side of Ruu. The children squatted beside them. All of them looked at the woman they had known all their lives.

Broda stood deep in thought over Rhae. He leaned on his crutch, rubbing the stump of his leg. As a hunter, he lived his life with death, accepting it and expecting it, but this death hurt him deeply. The death of Rhae, his lifelong friend, had happened too quickly. Time would heal his pain, eventually, but not now, not tonight, not while he still looked at her. She left him feeling helplessly mortal. He was not a man to look back at his life, but now, as he looked forward, his life felt short, too short. Shivering, he looked down at the hole in her chest. He touched his own chest, and shook his head. He could not remember seeing anything that looked like that wound. The thought passed quickly, he knew there was nothing he could do now but to help bury her.

The women carried baskets to the stream. The men, having dug the hole to their waists, climbed out. They threw dirt back into the hole to cover their footprints, then covered the bottom with leaves. The women returned with baskets filled with mud. The Tribe gathered around Rhae. Taking handfuls of mud, they covered her with it. Ruu tied the pouch to the True Knot around the neck of Rhae and laid it softly on her. Then, she gently covered the face with mud. The Tribe stood. The men lifted the bier. With her facing east, an eternity of sunrises, they lowered Rhae into her grave.

Klena stopped drumming. From out of the shadows, he walked quietly to the grave. He put the drum down. From his belt, he untied a small, beautifully decorated pouch. He lay on the ground and reached into the grave. He opened her hands. He placed a handful of mud in each palm. Opening his pouch, he selected two tiny seeds. Into each palm, he planted an apple seed.

The Tribe gathered around the grave. They scooped up handfuls of dirt and scattered them over Rhae. They filled the grave, knelt over it, and patted down the dirt. They took their bowls and walked to the stream. Three times, they returned to the grave and doused it with water. They knelt over it, patted down the mud, and scattered leaves on top.

Ruu took the wooden eating bowl of her mother, turned it over, and dug its lip deeply into the ground at the head of the grave. "Now, may you feel no hunger. You shall always have food. Now, may you feel no thirst. You shall always have water. Good-bye, Mother."

"Good-bye, Mother," repeated Krilu.

Klena rose slowly. He stared at the grave. Then, speaking softly, almost whispering, he said, "Life changes to death and changes again. Loved One, give life to those you leave behind. Do not forget us. Do not forsake us. Stay with us even as you leave. One last time we ask for your help. Become the growth that feeds the living. Become the hope that feeds our children and the children of our children. Grow and feed us, nurture and keep us. Become for us the food we need and your goodness, your beauty, and your love will forever taste sweet on our lips. Be fruitful and grow forever, Loved One."

From his pouch, Klena took out a small, bone flute. He played a heartfelt melody. His breath harmonized with the music, and together, they sounded like singing in a sighing breeze. He repeated the tune, each time softer and softer. Its hushed tones faded into the breeze. The breeze stopped. The last few notes whispered, then dissolved, into the still air. For one last moment, the Tribe sat with Rhae.

Klena put the flute back into his pouch. He picked up the drum. He stood, then the rest stood. They picked up the baskets and bowls. Families, holding hands, walked through the Grove. They kissed and hugged or simply stood under the apple trees growing over their dead relatives and friends.

CHAPTER 15

They left the Grove. The weary Tribe tramped groggily home as the moon neared the western horizon. The nocturnal animals crawled silently home to sleep. Walking Stream sounded tired as it crept along. The breeze had lost its strength and the trees hung listlessly in the predawn stillness.

The Tribe would not eat today. The loss of their anticipated meal of fresh elk meat only made them feel emptier. Tonight, the first full moon after the autumnal equinox, was the most sacred night of the year. Tonight was the Ceremony and no one ate on the day of the Ceremony.

Hsoro first spotted the prints. He said nothing, but walked more quickly. Traro joined him. He saw the prints, too. They led to the village.

The Tribe saw Hsoro and Traro walking faster. Krilu, rustling leaves, and Mekla, more quietly, moved up beside them. Sra and Mre slowed the children, separating them from the men. Ruu walked with Klena and Broda between the two groups.

"Wild dogs," whispered Broda.

There were more paw prints as they neared the village. Hsoro heard nothing. He stopped at the woods at the edge of the village, waited and listened.

"Help me! Where are you? Help!"

Hsoro and the men ran into the village. The center of the village was in shambles. From the oak tree hung an empty rope. Little was left from the elk quarter. Chewed lumps of meat were thrown about the village. Bones were crushed. Blood stained the ground.

Hsoro knelt over a gnawed piece of wood. Ruu knelt beside him. She also recognized the cane of Jascha. She ran to his hut. Near it, she found one of his moccasins, torn to shreds.

"I could have been killed! You do not care about me! I am helpless. I could have been killed. I am sick. Nobody cares about me!"

"All is well here," Mekla shouted down from the food shack.

Krilu returned from the storage hut. "They didn't get in. I wish I could have killed one of those dogs."

Broda limped toward the group. "They got the head. Tore it up. Must have been quite a pack of them. Damn scavengers!"

"Jascha?" Klena asked.

Ruu returned and said, "He is fine. He heard the wild dogs, got out of his hut, and tried to scare them away. They came after him. He threw his cane at them, then lost his moccasin as he crawled into his hut. He picked up a rock but the dogs forgot about him when they brought the meat down. He is fine but he is mad at himself for defending the village badly. He wants me to bring his cane, and to quiet Kru. Be quiet, Kru, it's over."

Traro returned from checking the huts. "All is safe," he said.

The Tribe was exhausted. Already, Sra and Mre held sleeping children. Other children, blinking and rubbing their half-closed eyes, leaned against their mothers. Some of the adults yawned widely, others stretched their tired arms and backs. The Tribe straggled to their huts and crawled inside. The village slipped into sleepy silence.

Almost imperceptibly, the eastern sky began to brighten.

Second Day

CHAPTER 16

Pale sunlight, falling through the oak tree, speckled the ground with shadows. The breeze touched a few leaves, scraping them across the ground. The breeze stopped and the leaves were still. Everything was still. The stillness of midday covered the village like shadows.

A crackling branch burst. A few sparks jumped into the cold air and disappeared. Ruu, holding the bloodstained deerskin hide of her mother, stared at the smoldering remains. Hsoro stood behind her. He laid his hands gently on her shoulders. The Tribe watched the smoke float away from the hut of Rhae. The sun slid behind a cloud and the shadows on the ground grew solid.

Ruu asked, "What killed my mother?"

"I will find out." Hsoro walked to his hut, took his sling and pebble pouch, his knife and sheath, and, without a word, walked into the woods.

Hsoro knew well the path that Rhae walked yesterday. His eyes glanced from tree to tree. He sniffed the air and felt the breeze. He listened carefully, walking quietly. He stopped. On the ground, a pool of dried blood, brownish and blending with the dirt, showed where Rhae died. He knelt, touched it lightly, then stood. He searched the ground for answers.

He took a step back, then another. His body stiffened. He grabbed his chest. He dropped to his knees, then fell forward. His chest rolled over the dried blood. His arms out flat, he pulled up two handfuls of weeds and dropped them. His toes dug into the ground. He barely breathed.

He lay still, then crawled to where he dropped the weeds. Lining up the weeds with his toe marks, he raised his eyes. Nothing looked suspicious. All he saw were thick growths of pine trees, too dense for a clear shot with a bow or spear.

"But there was no arrow or spear in Rhae."

He raised his eyes higher.

"There is a clear shot from there, but the distance is too far."

He looked far away at a large white boulder. He looked down at the dried blood on the ground, then again at the boulder. He shook his head. He looked for signs of lightning. There were none. He shook his head again as he stared at the faraway boulder.

He checked the ground as he walked to the boulder. Dead pine needles lay on the ground. There were no prints on them. He crawled under fallen tree trunks and over fallen branches. He pushed away branches that slapped at his face. Only grudgingly did the forest let him through.

"I played here as a child." Hsoro sighed when he reached the boulder. The white boulder, rounded and broken by time with a large crevice running down its face, was a huge conglomerate of black-speckled granite, crystalline quartz, and glistening mica. Hsoro climbed up. From the top, he could see clearly, far away, where Rhae died.

He untied his sling from his belt, opened his pebble pouch, and placed a pebble into his sling. He stepped forward and threw. The pebble dropped to the ground far short. As he took another pebble, he walked to the back of the boulder. He laid the pebble carefully into his sling. He ran across the boulder and threw with all his might. It fell short again. He shook his head as he turned the pouch on its side and rolled all the pebbles into his hand. Picking out one, he rolled the rest back into the pouch. He loaded his sling, then threw the pebble as high as he could. It cleared the first tree, but another tree caught it. After it bounced down through the branches and plopped on the ground, the forest was quiet.

Hsoro tied his sling back on his belt and walked to the back of the boulder. He looked down. The ground was pounded down hard. The grass was flattened. Hsoro lay down. He looked around and farther away from the boulder, then stared at something. He jumped off the boulder. Looking closely at the ground, he knelt.

"I have never seen any prints like this. It is wider than my hand and over twice its length. It is dug deep into the ground, yet it did not jump. It must weigh much. The print is almost flat. It is splay-footed, but it has no toes. The heel is dug deeper into the ground. It stands erect and it is big.

"What is it?"

Through the brambles, through the thickets, the dirt slid underfoot. Thorns tangled his way. Branches barred his way. Rocks jarred his bones. He turned this way and that way, winding his way up, unrelentingly upward. His mind wandered as Hsoro followed the tracks.

"What is it? It is alive and it walks on its feet. From where did it come? Why is it here? If it is like other animals, it comes, it is here, and that is all. But is it like me? Does it need to know? I need to know what it is. I must.

"Oh, why? Why all these questions? I must know, always I must know. Yet, even that is never enough. We who must know are never sure of what we know, while those who can feel can believe. But I do not have the gift of believing. Where is that one seed of knowledge that I can believe? Always I must search and search, perhaps finding truth for an instant, but then, I can only watch helplessly as it floats away. If only I could believe. But I cannot, and I am probably doomed not to know either. If only I knew what I needed to know. To search for something and yet not know what I am searching for is either the ultimate challenge or the ultimate folly. For me, it is my life. All else is incomplete and useless. All I may ever know is pain, frustration, and irreverence. The answers are as fleeting as smoke, and as unknowable. Is everything so unknowable?"

In the damp air filled with the scents of pines, a dim greenish haze hovered between the tall trunks. The large exposed roots of the pine trees crawled over the rocks, wrapping themselves silently around like old protective serpents. The dead and browning needles filled the cracks in the rocks and bark. Wrinkled rocks and furrowed bark lived together and waited in their time. Among the trees, saplings, with slender trunks, grew and waited for their days in the light. Dying, arching branches littered the ground. Cones and piles of cones lay together where they landed or rolled. Opened, their seeds gone to the animals or back to the earth to start the circle again. The earth never felt flat but always sliding underneath like something imaginably alive, and now with tracks on it and Hsoro following them.

"It goes in the same direction. The tracks are clear, it does not hide them. It is confident or foolish. It goes straight for the berry bushes, it does not circle them. It smashes its way through, breaking branches, uprooting plants. It is not gentle nor careful, it is powerful but not cautious. It goes where it wants not where the forest tells it.

"Are we only another animal with a hungry stomach? The animal that kills and cries. Does that make us better? We are not the only ones who feel. The other animals feel, too. The other animals nurture and protect, fear and love. What makes us different? Is it our empty stomach or our full skull? Our mind makes us think we are different. Our mind makes us crazy and mad, blind and closed to our true selves. It believes only in itself. And a world here only to serve it."

A crow swooped down at Hsoro. It barely missed his head, then flew away.

"The animals live only in the instant. When hungry, they eat. When tired, they sleep. They live and that is enough. That is so unlike us. We must struggle, we must push, we must accomplish and succeed. We must leave our footprints everywhere. We must hurry to devour the earth before she devours us."

A faint but definite trail twisted and turned and wound itself through the forest. The forest grew with a tangle of living, dying, and dead, intertwined and intermixed. A jumble of growth and mulch fed itself with its own remains. The tall trees survived until they grew old, tottered, and fell, and the younger trees grew through the rich, rotting mass on their vital journey to the light. Even at midday, the great cone-bearing forest stood gloomy and dark. Ferns, fungi, and mushrooms grew in this half-lit world of perpetual dusk. The light, broken, dispersed, and absorbed, rarely touched the ground. The thick, dark green needles hung still and silent. The wind moaned lightly overtop, but nothing moved on the forest floor except Hsoro, following the tracks.

"A pile, a large pile." Hsoro knelt. "It has eaten recently." He sniffed the pile. "It is a meat-eater, a large meat-eater." He picked the pile apart. "There is no fur in it. No bones, either. It does not eat all that it kills, but it eats much." Hsoro stood and walked on.

"Everything eats, and everything is food. We are all food. Life consumes life. We eat the animals and the plants, and the earth eats the animals, the plants, and us. We eat from the earth and the earth takes us back. We are food for others. We are part of the earth, not something above or beyond. There is no above or beyond, it is only a flattering, comforting lie. We go down, down and back to the earth, back to the beginning. We go back to the earth that gave us birth and gives birth to life for others to eat, for others to live. So it goes around and around. There is nothing higher than to give back all we have taken. We are nurtured and fed by the earth, and it is only right that we give back ourselves."

With its wings outstretched, the crow swooped down from out of the sun, blackening it. Hsoro crouched. The crow turned and dove again, screeching, then flew away.

"Is there more? I want to forever look like me, to forever be me. I cannot stand the thought of being eaten by bloodsuckers, maggots, and roaches. Is my life only a wait for that? There is more, there has to be more.

"A path, and it is much worn. It follows a path. There are prints in the other direction, too. The other tracks are older. They are from yesterday. It came and it went yesterday. It has not come today, yet."

Withered, dried, and pushed against the mountain, the stout pine trees, their bark ripped, their branches torn away, clung to the ground against the hard winds. The rocks, weathered, layered, and shattered, lay bare, breaking, crumbling, eroding to dust. Once they grew but we did not see that. Now they decay and we see that but slightly. Lichens ate from them and grew. Dried grass grew around their gravelly bottoms. Near one, a pile of dust partly hid an open burrow. Beside it lay the remains of a mouse, a meatless pile of fur and bones. Here lived a few mice and shrews, perhaps a raccoon or an oppossum. But with little to eat, the squirrels and chipmunks did not come here. Here the owls stalked, while the deer grazed and the wolves prowled. The path turned sharply up and Hsoro followed it.

"It stumbles and slides. It loses its balance. It walks unsteadily. It tires but does not stop, it pushes itself. It stays on its path. And it remembers.

"Can we not see our place on the earth without needing to place ourselves at the peak of all that exists? Why are we so superior? We are not so strong, we are not so swift, we are not so long-lived. We can change, yes, we can change. We can become something we were not in only a few generations. The earth changes and so do we. But if the earth does not change quickly enough for us, we try to change the earth. Then we grow sick, out of touch with the pace and rhythm of the earth. But is not the earth ours? The earth is here for us, or so we have learned to believe, or so we have flattered ourselves into believing. The earth smiles at our stupidity and laughs at our lies, and then, gathers us back into herself."

A screeching cry and a streak of blackness flew down at Hsoro. Hsoro dropped to the ground. "Go away!" Hsoro stood and the crow flew at him again. Hsoro waved his arms wildly. "Away!" It dove straight at him. An instant before its claws struck, Hsoro dove to the ground. Instinctively, his hand grabbed a sharp rock. He stood as it came again. He cocked his arm and threw. The rock hit the crow on the wing. Screaming loudly, it spun weakly to earth. Hsoro ran to find it. He found a few drops of blood, but not the crow. Hsoro fell to his knees and buried his face in his hands. "I can feel the scream of every creature I have ever killed.

"We are not gods. We are not angels. We are animals, incredibly interesting, fascinating, complex animals. Is that not enough? What more could we want? What more could we want except to ignore what we are? To become something else without knowing ourselves leads only down a path doomed to destruction, chaos, and madness.

"Where is it going? It hurries yet nothing chases it. There are no other tracks but its own. It hurries for food or shelter, or it is afraid. It is big, and it must need much food. Hungry, it would be weak. To be big and weak in the forest, and soon you are dead.

"I find comfort in joining the earth and in joining the others who came before. That something will grow out of me, something that will feed the living when my life is over, is a comfort for me. That is enough. Why would I want to exist somewhere else? We would probably maul that place, too. Such is our nature, to change, to alter our surroundings to please ourselves. Even if we cared, even if we tried to live within this world, our empty stomach and our full skull would not permit it. We demand change or death to everything that does not, cannot, or will not change for us. Our very existence changes everything. The other animals grow quiet and fearful because they do not trust us. Everything we touch, we destroy in the name of building a better world for ourselves. But the world was here long before us. Is it any better now?"

High on White Mountain, the squat and stunted tree clung tenaciously to the rocky ground. Twisted by the terrible battering of the harsh north winds and the unrelenting west winds, their deformed trunks and exposed roots looked frightening. The low scrub bushes, ragged and scraggly, rose from the ground like skeletal hands grasping fruitlessly at the incessant wind. Starved, dwarfed thickets grew bent and contorted against the mountain. The sparse weeds grew fitfully from the cracks between the rocks and from the gravel eroded by lichens and time. The ageless mountain sat still and silent. Securely, it sat in its eons of time. The rocks cracked and tumbled down and in a thousand generations the mountain might shrink the height of a child. Firmly, it sat with its deep core untouched by the hurried whims of living creatures. They grew and they died, they came and they went, while it sat and stayed. Gray clouds tumbled overhead and patches of light rolled up the mountain. The sun felt warm when it peeked out from behind the thick clouds. The rocks felt cold. The wind blew hard. Polished by the countless ages, by the ever-returning summer rains and winter snows, the rocky summit glowed like a jewel. Hsoro did not bother to look anymore for tracks.

"I know where you are going.

"I am no better than the ones who came before. I will make the same mistakes or different mistakes. The mistakes are within. The mistake is thinking we are better than what we are.

"Before, there were many more of us. Why are only we left?"

CHAPTER 17

Winter Valley spread before him like an opened hand. The dry grass looked flesh-colored and soft. Dark tree stumps and white rocks dotted the near side of the valley. Long River cut the valley in half. Red-leaved maple trees and golden birch trees filled the far side of the valley. Far in the distance, the four tree-filled gorges looked like fingers resting on the slope of the next mountain. The trees stopped abruptly against the bone-colored dome of the mountain. The Tribe rarely crossed Long River. No one had ever crossed over Unknown Mountain.

Hsoro walked down White Mountain. Creatures from another age died, disappeared into the ground, and grew into a mountain of marble. The scars and cliffs came later. The beautiful whiteness was stripped away. The marble was ripped out. The mountain was tortured, raped, then deserted. Gradually, warmed by the sun and welcomed by the bareness, small tufts of grass and tiny bushes came back. Birch trees wandered into the bareness. But nothing grew on the cliffs.

Hsoro climbed down the first cliff. Feeling tired and hungry, he carefully walked across the face of the cliff, checking his footing, moving his feet slowly, hoping the ledge would hold him and worrying that it would not. Near the bottom, the ledge narrowed. He could go no farther. With his belly flat against the cliff, he pushed off, turned in the air, and landed firmly on the rocky ground.

Down the next cliff, the footing felt slippery and Hsoro felt shaky. The ledge narrowed, then disappeared. Higher than he hoped, he turned, searched the ground, and jumped. The ground slid underfoot. He fell down hard. His head hit the cliff. The ground slid under him. He dug his feet into the earth. He slid down with the moving ground. Dirt kicked up into his face. Stones rolled over him. He rolled over. He slid down to the next cliff. Face down, his feet fell over the cliff. He slid over a rock. His face dragged over it. He grabbed the rock. It stopped him. The far end of the rock lifted up and its front end dragged nearer to the edge. His legs waved helplessly against the cliff as the rock slid closer. Dirt showered down into his eyes and mouth. The rock rolled over the edge. Hsoro dropped onto a ledge. The rock hit him on his back and slammed him against the cliff. With a crash, the rock hit the ground far below and tumbled into the bushes. Pressing himself against the cliff, Hsoro crept down the ledge until he safely reached the bottom. At the bottom, he slid into the soft dirt and rested.

Vultures circled over Winter Valley. With their huge black wings outstretched, naked necks extended, bare red heads steady, they searched the valley. On the near side of the valley, more vultures, screeching at each other with their wings flapping loudly, squatted on the tree stumps. Others walked awkwardly on the ground, fighting among themselves. Some rushed headlong to a spot and pushed the weaker ones away, pecking them. Around the larger groups, lone scavengers searched the ground. One picked up something and, with its head bent back, gulped it down.

Hsoro leaned his back against the bottom of the cliff. He felt groggy as he got up. His stomach growled. Dirt covered his face and stuck to his bleeding scratches. He picked dirt out of his disheveled hair as he walked down.

He climbed down the next cliff easily. The cliffs were smaller and the plateaus between them grew wider. Grass and the passing of ages turned the stone to dust and dirt. The rains and the ages smoothed the ground. The golden-leaved birch trees filled the ground more fully. From here, the way down was easy. Hsoro knew well the path down White Mountain. It led to the Winter Cave.

Something across the path caught his ankle. It felt heavy. He took a step back and let it down. It made a strange clinking sound. Black links interlocked along its length. "A chain?"

One end of it was attached to the trunk of a birch tree. Its other end was attached to something in the leaves. The leaves around it were scattered wildly. A black half-circle stuck out ankle high. He knelt down. Dried blood was scattered around it and on it. Fur was stuck to the blood. A severed leg of an animal, a cat, stuck out of it.

The black thing felt cold and slick. He tapped it with his fingers. It felt solid, dense, and hard. He shook his head. "Metal?"

The sharp teeth of the thing were clamped shut. He tried to pull them open. He couldn't. Two metal spikes pounded into the ground held it down. He tugged hard and pulled it out of the ground. He shook his head again. "A trap."

He let it drop from his hands. Cracked like a twig by the force of the trap, the broken leg of the cat stuck up emptily. The top of its leg was chewed off. Drops of blood led to the bushes. The animal did not get far. He smelled it before he saw it. The putrid smell of rotting flesh made him feel sick.

He found the carcass nearby. "It must have died in great pain, but it so loved its freedom that it chewed off its own leg rather than die in a trap."

Its beautiful fur was stripped away. The meat was left to rot. The sight of wasted meat made him sick. He found straight cut marks on the skin. "The fur is cut off, but the throat is not slit." The blank eyes of the dead lynx stared up at Hsoro.

Footprints were everywhere. Hsoro followed them. They led back to the path. "I am close." He wanted no more prints showing, so he walked in the prints of the other. "It has large strides." He stretched his short legs, occasionally jumping from print to print. He stayed in the tracks. What looked like one set of prints now hid another and only he could tell, he hoped.

To the ragged edge of the last cliff, he crawled on his belly. He searched the valley. Nothing moved suspiciously. He listened. He heard nothing suspicious. Cautiously, he started down.

The white marble face of the cliff crumbled from the passing of time. Age cracked its face. The wind, rain, and snow scratched it, too. Broken by droplets of water, freezing and thawing, huge boulders dropped down. Slowly, almost unnoticed, the cliff slid into rocks, stones, and pebbles, into dirt, dust, and the valley. From the cragged face of the cliff, shadows fell into the valley, over the boulders, into the Cave, over Hsoro.

The shaded cliff felt cold. Hsoro shivered on it. Lichens grew on the rocks and moss grew on the lichens and a few stunted, leafless trees hung desperately to the bare rock. Dead, moss-covered twigs littered the ledge. The ledge dropped down sharply, leveled off, then dropped down again. Hsoro walked down large steplike cuts and across broad ledges cut into the cliff. The ledge stopped. He knelt down. "This break is new."

He stepped back and jumped over it. A cliff swallow shot out of a

crevice above his head. Hsoro slipped, but swiftly regained his footing. A stone bounced down the cliff and plopped in front of the Cave.
"Not far now." He continued down. His hands felt cold and stiff.
His legs felt weak. He dropped to the ground and quickly hid behind
a large boulder.

CHAPTER 18

The Tribe had rolled the large boulders away from the mouth of the Cave. Encircling a clearing, the boulders protected the Tribe from the harsh winter winds and kept blowing snow from burying the mouth of the Cave. Across the clearing from the Cave grew two maple trees. The northern tree, Once-a-year tree, guided the sun up on the shortest day of the year. The southern one, Twice-a-year tree, guided the sun up on the morning they left for the village and the morning after the Ceremony.

Between the trees, they could see Winter Valley. On the near side of Long River, they had cut down most of the trees, opening up this side of the valley for grass and shrubs. This provided the foraging animals with food and the hunters with animals. In the spring, the Tribe had cut down some trees for the coming winter and stacked the wood beside the boulders to dry while they were gone. While at the village, rarely did anyone come here.

While at the Cave, rarely did anyone go far from it. A sudden snowstorm, rolling over the mountains, could kill. Hsoro disliked hunting far from the valley. But when desperate he approved because he felt he must do something. Only Traro and he hunted away from the valley. Together, they climbed White Mountain. Sometimes they brought back a muskrat or a hare, but, more often, they returned empty-handed, and cold, hungry, and exhausted. During the winter, the best place for hunting was from the clearing in front of the Cave.

When they could, they escaped from the confining Cave. The children cleaned the clearing to keep away scavengers. The women unearthed meat frozen in pits beneath the clearing. The men searched the valley for food. They found animals, starved, dead, and frozen. They killed animals, weakened by the hard winter. Always, the Tribe watched for scavengers and animals. Everything they found or killed, they ate.

The cool air reeked of rotting flesh. Hsoro covered his mouth as he stood and leaned against a boulder. Pelts of deer and rabbits, raccoons and beavers covered the boulders. Usually, grass grew on the gravelly clearing, but there were only footprints. Stains of crushed berries and blood scarred the ground. On the clearing lay bones, with meat still on them, uncracked for their marrow. Maggots crawled over the meat, spoiling on the ground. Beautiful blue feathers crept away in the breeze from a dead bluebird.

At the hearth in the center of the clearing, ashes half-covered a large black pot. Hsoro knelt. He touched the ashes. They were cool. He touched the pot. It was icy cold. "Metal."

He leaned over and looked inside. Burnt food crusted it. A pair of cockroaches crawled onto his hand. He shook them off. Grime covered his palms.

"CAAA!" Hsoro whirled around. In front of the Cave, a bluejay calmly picked up a berry, gulped it down, screamed again, and flew away. Hsoro stared at the mouth of the Cave. He stood and walked quickly and quietly to the boulders, and behind them to the cliff. He edged against the cliff and to the Cave. He stopped within reach of its mouth and smeared the soot from his palms over his face.

He listened, but heard nothing. He tried to calm himself, but still shivered. On his thigh, he wiped the sweat off his left hand. He unsheathed his knife. He took a deep breath and ran into the Cave.

The darkness swallowed him. He tripped over something. It clanged as he fell to the ground. His knife slipped from his hand. He crawled back until he touched the wall. He could see nothing. He could do nothing, but hide, and wait.

The cool walls sweated and Hsoro sweated. Everything felt dense and close. He swept his hand in front of him, feeling for his knife. He felt something cold and pulled his hand back. The rough rock rubbed against his back as he pushed himself against the wall. The darkness hid him. He waited for his eyes to adjust to the darkness.

A half-oval of gray light spread into the Cave from its mouth. Gradually, shapes appeared in the darkness. A dark half circle stuck up near him. Another trap, with its teeth wide open, stuck into the ground near his head. Lumps and strange shapes littered the ground. Antlers stuck up like bare bushes. On the ground, bones were scattered and rolled pelts were piled. A ring of stones circled a hearth and a leg of an animal, burnt, hung from the spit. A bone stuck out of the ashes. A pelt laid, unrolled, beside the hearth.

Footprints were dug deeply into the damp dirt. Hsoro reached out his hand and found his knife. He cleaned the stone blade on his thigh and wiped the sweat off his face.

Crouching low, he crept along the wall. At the opening to a chamber off the main cave, he stopped. He waited and listened. In the winter, they kept dried food and thawed meat here. Holding his knife tightly, he stepped inside. Bones littered the chamber and a pile of pelts laid against the far wall. Hsoro leaned against the opening and slid to the ground.

He could see in the dark now, but so could anything else. He crawled across the Cave, avoiding the light from the outside. The ceiling above the hearth was black with soot. He crouched beside another opening. They kept dried wood here. He heard nothing. He stepped inside. A dead twig snapped and leaves crunched under his foot. He wiped the sweat off his hands as he left.

He sidled farther into the Cave, toward another opening. Here the women gave birth. They hung hides over the opening. A fire warmed the chamber and a pot of water. The women knelt over the pregnant woman. She lay on hides on the ground. A knife laid beside her. She used the knife to cut the cord, and again, if she decided to kill the baby. If she, and the two women, decided the baby was well, they washed the baby and cooked the afterbirth. The shaman came and examined the baby. He rarely decided against a baby. The shaman told her mate. The man was not allowed to see her until after she ate. He was not allowed to see the baby until after it suckled. If it did not suckle, then the baby died.

Hsoro held his knife tightly. He heard rustling inside. He crawled in. Leaves were piled against the far wall. A rat looked up from her nest, grabbed her baby by the back of its neck, and dove into the leaves. Hsoro turned and crept out.

He edged deeper into the Cave. The ceiling slanted down. He crawled on the damp ground to the end of the Cave. It felt stuffy and cramped. He touched a pile of rocks. Bare teeth of a bear skull grinned at him. "I am alone."

He turned and slumped against the rocks hiding the opening to the Initiation Cave. Hidden by the darkness, he breathed a sigh of relief and laid his knife on his lap. Wrapping his hide snuggly around himself, he rested and his mind wandered back to his twelfth year and to his Initiation.

"A torch sticks into the ground. The cave is small. The air smells of earth. I lay naked on the ground. The ground is damp and rocky. The rocks stick into my back. Klena kneels beside me and, with a sharp stone, cuts my palms. He lifts my hands over my face. 'See the liquid? Inside the solid is liquid, inside the body is blood. Inside the liquid is air, inside the blood is spirit.' Drops fall on my lips. 'Breathe deeply, young one, and feel the spirit flow through you.' Klena takes the torch and crawls out. He piles rocks over the opening. 'Dream while awake. Think while asleep. In the darkness, you will find yourself.' The last rock stops the light.

"I am alone. I am afraid. I do not move. The oppressive darkness of the unknown holds me. My heartbeat echoes from the wall. The floor feels hard. I shiver uncontrollably. I want to run. My mind is restless. My mind runs like a panicked animal. It runs and runs, hitting the walls, howling and screaming. It runs for twelve years, in the sun and snow, through the streams and forest, with my friends and family, hearing the carefree laughter of other children, feeling the delight of smooth pebbles in my hands, smelling the cooking fire and tasting the food. It crawls exhausted back to the cave. It cowers against the wall, panting like an animal, then falls asleep.

"Eyes stare at me. From everywhere, eyes stare at me. Old eyes, deep eyes, silent eyes. Warmth fills the cave. I look around. The cave is shut. I look around. The cave is empty. Eyes, two by two, reappear. The cave grows warmer. The bright eyes nod up and down in the darkness. One pair of eyes comes toward me. They stare at me. They come closer. They are mine. I want to close my eyes but I do not know which are mine. I stare at my eyes and my eyes stare at me. I feel dizzy and helpless. From out of the eyes come people, faces, swarms of faces. Everyone is different. All are strangers. Faces of strangers come toward me, around me, pass me. I cry. I cannot touch them. I cannot know who they are. But as they pass me, each one makes me warmer. Sweat flows from my body. I feel like liquid. The last of them passes me.

"The cave lightens. The walls disappear. I feel weightless. The cave glows. I see a body, glistening in the light. It is mine. It looks strange and out of place. It no longer holds me. I float in the lightness. I fly. A streak of light falls across my body. The cave grows darker as the light grows wider. I hear the voice of Klena. 'You have done well, Hsoro.' He takes my hand and touches my fingers lightly on my belly, right shoulder, forehead, left shoulder, and belly. 'You and the circle are one.'

"He leads me out of the Initiation Cave and carries me out of the Winter Cave and down to Long River. He wades in and dips me into the water. 'You are one of us.' He hugs me. We hold each other as we walk back to the Winter Cave."

Hsoro touched his belly, shoulder, forehead, shoulder, and belly.

CHAPTER 19

A stone bounced down the cliff and plopped in front of the Cave. It startled Hsoro. He stared, through the darkness, through the dim light at the mouth of the Cave, at the clearing. "It comes."

Hsoro put his knife away. He opened his pebble pouch, felt the smooth pebbles, and loaded his sling. He crawled toward the mouth of the Cave. He heard nothing. Avoiding the light from the outside, he stayed hidden in the darkness. He crouched against the wall. Staying still, he waited and listened. He checked his grip on his sling. He waited, but heard nothing. He nodded his head and took a deep breath. "Now!"

He ran out the Cave, dove, and rolled to the side. He crouched against the cliff. His eyes glanced over the familiar clearing, boulders, trees. "Nothing." He sighed and leaned back against the cliff.

His eyes widened as he felt the rock against his back. He patted the cliff and nodded to himself. Pushing himself against the cliff, he turned his head and looked up. The overhanging cliff hid the ledge. He crept carefully along the cliff, then behind the boulders. He crawled past the first one, then the second. Behind the third, he hid. On his knees, he turned and faced the cliff. He listened, but heard nothing. He felt the weight of his loaded sling in his left hand. Slowly, he raised his head until he could see the cliff, then the ledge.

An arrow pointed straight at his eyes. Behind it, a big man held a drawn bow.

"Hsoro!" The man lowered his bow.

"Traro!"

"Did you find it?"

"No. Did you?"

"No."

"Can you see it?"

Traro searched the valley from the ledge on the cliff. "No."

Hsoro stood, leaned against the boulder, and shook his head.

"Come!" Traro waved his bow at Hsoro. "It is late. We must get back."

Hsoro nodded his head and started climbing up the cliff.

"Look at you." With a big smile, Traro greeted Hsoro. "I have not seen you so dirty since we were children." He patted Hsoro on his back and a cloud of dirt popped around his hand. "I cannot take you back like this." Laughing, Traro good-naturedly pummeled Hsoro until dirt covered both of them.

Hsoro smiled, then began to run. "Hurry, we must not be late."

Suddenly, he stopped. He stood for a moment and scratched his head. Leaning over the ledge, he looked down. "The wood is gone."

Traro looked down, too. "Where could it be?"

"I do not know."

"Maybe, it's a giant beaver?"

"What?"

Traro shrugged his shoulders.

"I do not know what it is, Traro. I do not know."

The men ran up White Mountain together.

"It's big," Traro said.

"The Cave is a mess."

"It's strong."

"It is thoughtless."

"It's powerful."

"It is wasteful."

"I wish I could have seen it," said Traro, "perhaps, I would feel better."

"I know I would feel better," said Hsoro.

The huge red sun pulled down the blue from the sky. In the darkening sky, a few fluffy clouds floated. Their wrinkled bottoms blazed scarlet, their shredded tops glowed orange. Silhouetted against the sun, far away, geese flew south. The sun trembled as it touched the horizon. Surrounded by a sunset burning the sky, Hsoro and Traro, blinded, shielded their sensitive eyes. Quietly, Hsoro said, "It is a good night for the Ceremony."

They walked down into the dusk. The darkness gathered in their shadows.

CHAPTER 20

Klena bent down. The last armload of dried cedar wood slid from his arms and rattled loudly as it rolled toward the large woodpile in the center of the Ground. He stacked the wood against the pile. Rubbing the scar on his forehead, he circled the Ground, examining everything again. He turned away and, without a word, walked into the woods.

The sun rolled out from behind thick white clouds, staining the woods yellow as its light fell through the leaves. Klena rested against a birch tree. Its swaying trunk pushed against his back as the wind shook the branches overhead. Catching a strip of bark and pulling it from the tree, the matted fur of his hide exposed the soft green trunk underneath as Klena walked away.

A gray squirrel, with its jowls filled, looked back over its shoulder as it scampered on the path ahead of Klena. The wind gusted. Brittle leaves fell around him.

"Watching the leaves fall makes me feel sad. Watching the animals store away their food and knowing that so many of them will not live to see another spring makes me feel sad. The days shrink and the world settles down to its winter sleep. Many will not awake. The animals must know this, too. Their minds are set on food and work. Everything is deadly serious. Everything, every living thing must watch for what it must have. The season is harsh and the minds of those awake must be harsh, too.

"I am hungry. I, too, need food. Always, I need food. I never used to get this hungry. I used to be able to go for days without food and without pain. I cannot do that any more. I am old. Before, my years seemed long and my days I filled laughing at the face of death. I cannot do that any more. Now, my days are short and my years have too few days. Too much time has piled on me. Time is a burden on me and I must carry it. The world feels heavy on me. I am not so strong any more. There is too much past that I must carry with me, but that is what I must do. Tonight is the Ceremony. I know this will be my last. I want my family and friends to remember me. This is my way of defying the impermanence in this world. Tonight, I will do what I know I can still do."

Klena stopped where Rhae died. He knelt and touched the dried blood. "I could not save the leg of Broda and I could not help you. Rhae, you called me a good shaman. But I cannot help anyone. We will not be apart long. I have lived long enough to die. Growing old is hard to accept. Answer me, Rhae, is death easier to accept?"

The whistling wind swept through the forest, whipping the sagging grass down, whirling the tumbling leaves around. The straining trees groaned. Leaves smacked against leaves and slapped against trunks. Pine cones dropped, bounced, rolled, and stopped against piles of pine needles. The cold wind stopped. The trees bent less and less. The leaves shivered but hung onto the swaying branches. The grass stood up again. Klena stood up, too. Hearing another gust of wind pushing through the forest, he bundled himself in his hide as he walked on.

"What has happened to the dreams of my youth? There were so many things I was going to do, to change, to accomplish. Oh, my dreams were grand. My accomplishments are meager. I have not always had the strength I would have liked. Perhaps if I had been stronger or more persistent, I would have succeeded. Was I wrong to dream? The world seemed fresh and new, and everything seemed possible. But the longer I lived the more I learned that not everything was possible. I feel cold. I feel cold and empty and the emptiness inside me grows. I find myself shivering for no reason. My hands tremble when they should be steady. My legs shake when they should be firm. My mind wavers, comes and goes as it pleases. My heart feels heavy and sinks into the emptiness. More and more, I feel I do not have the strength to pull my heart out of the emptiness.

"Come on, old man, stop this shaking! It is not that cold and you should not be that tired. There is work to do, work to keep you busy. You insult yourself by worrying about what is to come when you have work yet to do here. Come on, old man, come on! Keep going!"

The path twisted and turned, climbing over boulders, sliding under fallen trunks, narrowing until it nearly disappeared only to widen again a few strides ahead. Klena stayed on the path. The path climbed steeply. Once bright red, the brown leaves of maple trees crunched underfoot. The creeping shadows and rushing wind chilled him. The wind swirled through the trees, pushing the leaves and Klena. The shadows trembled on the rough ground.

"The world looks so much different to me now. It has changed much. But change is the way of things. Birth to growth to decay to death. It all happens so fast. I am fortunate to have lived out my life. Nine out of ten animals never know the bitter pleasure of growing old. It is painful this growing old. I watch an unconcerned world spin around and around and an overconcerned man spin down and down. I feel tired. Everything has changed too much for me. The changes no longer excite me. They hurt."

Klena stopped where the path split in two. Ahead, it faded and disappeared into the undergrowth. To his side, it led into Stone Meadow. He stared into Stone Meadow and at the white, tumbledown stones in it. "I remember when they stood in neat, orderly rows. I wish I knew what the worn writing on them meant."

The sun gleamed down on the discolored stones and faded sunflowers.

"I am tired of the changes. I am of the old ways. The ways of the young are not my ways. They are the ways of others and I am forced to accept them as elders, always, were forced to accept changes they neither approved of nor understood. Now, I, too, do not bend easily in the new breezes. I am not young anymore. I cannot walk so far nor think so well anymore. I cannot pass my time with my friends, I have buried too many of them. I have seen too many deaths and I am tired of it. Can you hear me, Rhae? I am tired of death. I am tired of burying my friends. Soon, I may be too tired to accept death in my own way."

CHAPTER 21

Klena pushed on. The path narrowed, then disappeared into the undergrowth. Branches slapped at him. Pine needles stuck to his hands. He pushed away a branch. It slipped from his hand and hit his face.

"By my strength and will, I was going to change this world. Yet, it seems little changed for all my efforts. I have struggled and worked hard to leave a path of myself through this world. Oh, if only I had known that our paths disappear so soon."

He stooped under thick branches. Rough branches scratched at his sweating skin. He climbed up and over a dirty rock and slid down its side. Mosses stained his breeches. He crawled under a fallen tree. Seeds stuck to his hide. Pine needles squished underfoot as he walked on.

"I have lived a long time and I have watched my beliefs change. What I once held so dearly I no longer believe and what I once did not grasp I now believe. If everything stayed the same, oh, how much easier it would be. What was right once would always be right and what was wrong once would always be wrong. But that is not the way of this world. Paths disappear under the snow. The forest takes back paths that are not used. Water floods what once we walked on. Boulders fall on our paths and we are too weak or too tired or too busy with our daily lives to move them, and so, our paths change. Old familiar paths disappear within a lifetime; within a lifetime old familiar paths disappear many times, until we are not even sure there were any paths at all. It is hard to remember old paths, and even harder to open new ones. I am old and tired. It is for the young and brave to open new paths. I will honor the old paths."

Tumbling clouds covered the sun. The sunlight faded. Creeping out from the vanishing shadows, the hidden, gentle greeness of the forest swelled in the cool shade. The many-hued mosses on the rocks and trunks, and the ferns around their bottoms, and the grasses sweeping between them, glowed with a light all their own. Long-leaved vines swung. Bowers of branches danced in the breeze. The breeze stilled. The sunlight brightened. As the sun slipped out from behind the rolling clouds, the colors of the forest dimmed and the stark shadows darkened. In a field, in the bright sunlight, Klena shielded his weak eyes.

A red-tailed hawk circled in the sky. Its shadow circled on the field. The hawk turned and swooped down. The hawk and its shadow met over a running rabbit. The shadow ran across the field as the hawk soared high above Klena.

"Why cannot I accept the world for what it is? Why cannot I accept that the world is beyond my control? I cannot change the world. Changing the world will not make it right for me. The world will only be right for me when I can see it with its eyes, see it for what it truly is. I can only change the way I live my own life. I have to accept that my time is limited, that what I can do for others is limited, and that what I can do to myself is limited. I am bound to my human ways. No matter how hard I struggle to stretch my bonds, I am bounded by myself."

Klena walked slowly across the open field. Old trees around its edges leaned in, grasping at the life-giving light. Young trees took to the open field and stretched up to the sky, rending and outgrowing their restricting bark. The roots of the young trees spread farther and farther each year that Klena made his pilgrimage here. Each year, more of the old trees fell down as the young ones crept in from out of the thick forest, bringing back with them the darkness of the forest.

Tall, tangled weeds covered the field and the slope rising gently before him. Under his feet, the gravel path crunched loudly. Weeds grew around, through, and over the fallen walls of an abandoned stone house. He walked through the opening between the low, crumbling walls. The concrete floor felt stiff and hard. Dandelions grew from between the wide cracks in the floor. Resting his hand against the flat, mossy green stones of the wall, he walked to the far end of the house, to where a rickety chimney, barely standing, sagged. He brushed away cobwebs from the stone ledge in front of the familiar fireplace and sat down. The mortar between the stones had long ago worn away. One of the stones had fallen off the ledge and cracked on the floor since Klena was last here, the day of the Ceremony last year.

"The world will go on without me. It will be little changed by me. It is as if I have spent my life pushing the wind. The wind blows at its own pace. The world changes at its own pace. My years are little to the time and patience of this world. Maybe, I made the world a little better, made my family and friends a little happier. I had always hoped that as I got older, the purpose for my life would become more clear, but it has only gotten more muddled."

Cuddling small clouds between them, large white clouds with soft shaded bottoms floated overhead like a family and friends out for a late afternoon stroll through the blueness. Wispy cloaks of pale clouds covered them as they nuzzled one another. The sunlight drifted down, brightening their fluffy heads as they nodded gently across the sky. Rising and dipping, turning and moving to and fro, never still, always changing, they rode quietly on the high wind over the spinning earth. The clouds looked exactly like clouds, nothing more or less, beautiful clouds, separate and together with the wind and the blueness above and the earth and a lone old man below.

"Living so long has made me dizzy. Spinning earth, spinning seasons, spinning days, is it any wonder that I grow dizzy? Stumbling through life in a stupor, few of us ever understand its changes. We think we are the gusting wind, stopping far away from where we started, carrying great waves of seeds with us, changing whatever we touch. In our dizzy comings and goings, the calm stillness of the earth confuses us. I long for the slow, gentle rhythms of the earth."

The wind whispered quietly inside the fireplace. Klena crawled inside, crossed his legs, pulled his hide around himself, and sat.

Inside the chimney, in a protected corner halfway up, a family of mud-dauber wasps had built a nest. The female circled Klena as the male flew by carrying a spider. He laid the paralyzed orb-weaver spider at the mouth of one of the cells of the nest. She, ignoring the intrusion of Klena, flew up to the nest. She took the spider and pulled it into the chamber where she had laid her eggs, where in the spring the growing larvae would eat the spider. He flew away to hunt again. The wasp crawled out and, having taken care of the food needed for her children, children she would never live to see, carefully sealed the cell to protect them.

A fat, hairy, woolly bear caterpillar, crawling across the fireplace in front of Klena, stopped. She turned, raised her head, and eyed Klena, particularly the thick, hairy hide wrapped around him. She crawled to the edge of the hide and carefully pulled a single hair from it. The caterpillar crawled back across the stones and climbed the wall of the chimney. Two large black stripes and a narrow brown stripe between them wiggled as she climbed. She laid the hair on her cocoon, moved it once, then turned around and crawled down in search of another hair for her home as she continued to prepare for the winter, and for living.

"It is strange that what was once so important to me is not so important anymore. Oh, I would have died for my dreams. But, I lived and I grew old and I grew to know that it is more important to live, to live to do the many small deeds that fill this life. Living is quite enough for this life. Life is not for glorious deaths over dreams, but for ordinary living, day by day, doing those small deeds that fulfill this life. There has been too much dying for dreams both grand and futile. This is a good time for living, for awake and ordinary living."

He touched his belly, right shoulder, forehead, left shoulder, and belly.

CHAPTER 22

Klena took a deep breath and crawled out of the fireplace. He walked away from the house, over the gravel path, across the field, and toward home.

"I am comfortable with my life. I am at home with the turnings of this world and with the comings and goings of the seasons. Nothing looks ugly or out of place. Nothing I will do will make this world any more or less beautiful. To live, that is enough meaning for this life, that is enough of an accomplishment. There was so much that I wanted to do and it was all out of proportion with what I could do. There is so little that I want to do now, and perhaps, that, too, is all out of proportion with what I can still do.

"Slow down, sun! I am an old man and I can walk only so fast. I am on my way home. Perhaps I did linger too long today but I had much to do to prepare myself. Tonight is very important for me. Today is important for you, but you will have many more days. Your time is endless. My time is not. Please, trees, do not block my way! You can linger much longer than I can. Your world changes slowly. Your time and my time are different. I can see in myself the changes that time has wrought and that this world changes beyond my control. Does that make all I have done and worked so hard for go for naught? I hope not. My time was good. The changing world does not change the good I have done. Others may not remember the good I have done but I can do nothing about that. I can only do so much."

The quiet water of Small Creek flowed down gently. The water followed the bends in the mountain and the path followed the bends in the creek. Klena walked on the path beside the burbling water. A brown leaf, its feathery, fragile veins showing through, floated by. The leaf touched a rock, spun around, and floated on unharmed. Two veined hands, cupped together, brought cool water to a thirsty Klena, kneeling beside the creek.

"The world rolls on like a great river, much too powerful for a little man like myself. Perhaps all the Tribe will die and there will be no more of us, but I have given some people an opportunity to live out their lives. That is enough for one person for one lifetime. I can do no more. I can do no more but accept what I have been able to do and not grieve for what I could not do."

Round, worn pebbles dotted the shore. Klena picked up a smooth pebble. He smiled at the soft feel that time had given to its hardness. He laid the pebble back where he found it and started down again.

"The changes I dreamed of doing to this world, the world has done to me. The changes have taken place inside of me. No one can see them. Yet trying to show them to others is still my dream. My dreaming has never stopped."

The path widened and leveled off, sloping smoothly at the bottom of Broad Mountain. The relaxing greenness, the comforting light from the golden-leaved birch trees, and the soft colors of dusk soothed his tiredness. A gray squirrel with its jowls filled looked back over its shoulder as it scampered on the path ahead of him.

Klena rested against a birch tree at the edge of the village. Rubbing the scar on his forehead, he looked out over the Ground. Then he looked up at the sky. The last red sliver of sun slid below the horizon.

"It is not easy this growing old. Yet, each day I cannot help but feel happy to be alive. No matter how much or how little I have accomplished in my life, my life has mattered. I believe that in the hearts of my children and my friends, they would agree that my life has mattered. Perhaps I did not change the world. The world is big and I am small and not all who have changed the world have changed it for the better. But amongst my children and my friends, I can see how my life has mattered. I have helped them when I could, and sometimes when I could not. I have accepted their help when I needed it, and have accepted, too, when I could not be helped. I have even accepted their help when I did not need it because we need to help as well as to be helped. I have always shared with others when I had it, and sometimes when I did not. I have shared, too, the hunger and anguish when there was nothing to share. Most important, I have always tried to give love and compassion to my children and my friends, and to accept love and compassion from them. I have not always succeeded, but I have often tried. After all, it is the trying in this life that matters."

CHAPTER 23

Klena walked onto the Ground. He circled the Ground to the east, to the south, to the west. At the north, he stopped. Standing on a large bearskin rug laid on the dirt, he stripped naked. He sat down with his back to the north and crossed his legs. He faced the large woodpile.

In front of the rug and to his side, Klena moved his wooden bowl filled with water and red clay.

On the rug, to his left, lay a short bow; a long, flat piece of wood; a short, round piece of wood; and a strip of birch bark with dried grass. Beside them lay a willow stick, as long as his forearm, sharpened at its top, blunted at its bottom. To his right lay a shorter birch stick with its bark removed and its wood carefully prepared. Next to it lay a special pouch. Behind him sat a clay pitcher filled with fresh water.

The Tribe had washed themselves carefully, except Hsoro and Traro who had returned too late to bathe. Under their deerskin robes, all were naked. Excited and anxious, the Tribe sat in a circle around the woodpile.

Outside the circle, Klena had earlier pounded four green spicebush sticks into the Ground, one for each direction. Inside where they sat, he had heaped a circle of multicolored leaves around the woodpile. The Tribe placed their wooden bowls between themselves and the leaves. Each bowl was filled with water and red clay.

Klena moved the flat piece of wood in front of him. He held the plank down between his bare feet and slid the strip of birch bark against the plank. On the bark he laid dried grass. He picked up the short bow and checked its knot by pulling on its buckskin strap. The knot felt firm. Picking up the long willow stick, he wrapped the taut strap around it once. The small, rounded piece of oak with a shallow hole worn into its middle, he held in the palm of his hand. Rubbing some fat into the hole, he put the piece of oak against the pointed end of the stick. The blunted, blackened end of the stick he pushed into a hole in the middle of the plank.

Beginning slowly, he pulled and pushed the bow back and forth, evenly, parallel to the plank. The strap groaned. The stick squeaked as it rubbed against the plank. A tiny wisp of smoke curled up toward him. He rose to his knees, leaned over, and pushed down harder. He pulled and pushed the bow faster. The stick squeaked louder against the plank and darker smoke rose. He pulled the stick out of the hole and breathed on the end of it. The stick glowed brightly. He blew lightly on it again as he bent over and brought it down to the dried grass. Curling and rushing away from the glowing stick, bits of grass sparked. He blew again. The stick glowed more brightly. He pushed the stick in deeper. A small blade of grass jumped into flame and ran back to another blade. The second blade glowed. Another blade caught fire. Gently, Klena picked up the fire growing in the grass. He cradled it in his hands. He breathed softly into it. Soft smoke rose from between his hands. A tiny flame flickered as he rose to his feet. Klena raised his hands silently toward the sunset, glowing bright amber in the west. Carefully, he walked to the woodpile. He laid the small flame into the center of the pile among the dried grass, bits of bark, and small twigs that he had arranged for it. The little flame settled into the grass and grew, burning the bark, then the twigs.

"The fire starts again," Klena whispered.

He turned away from the fire, toward the growing darkness, and walked back to the rug. He moved the bow, plank, and rounded piece of wood to the side. He picked up the long willow stick, turned, and pushed its blunted end into the fire.

"Look," said Klena, "the fire is rising again, catching hold of the wood. The fire burns brightly. Gold is the first age of fire."

He pulled the glowing stick from the fire. He turned around with his arms outstretched. "We offer this Ceremony to the horizon for sheltering us."

He pointed the stick to the sky. "We offer this Ceremony to the sky for covering us."

He pointed the stick to the earth. "We offer this Ceremony to the earth for feeding us."

He pushed the stick into the fire, waited until it burned again, then pulled it out. He walked outside the circle and, facing east, drew a bright gold circle in the darkness. "To the east, to the morning."

"We are here," the Tribe said.

He stopped in the south and drew a gold circle in the darkness. "To the south, to the summer."

"We are here."

He stopped in the west and drew a circle in the darkness. "To the west, to the evening."

"We are here."

He stopped on the rug and drew a circle toward the north. "To the north, to the winter."

"We are here."

He turned to the fire and circled the stick above his head. "To above, to the day."

"We are here."

He lowered the stick to the ground. "To below, to the night."

"We are here."

He pointed the stick to the fire. "To life, to us."

"We are here."

He pointed the smoldering stick to each of the green sticks in the four directions. "The sticks are the wind that surrounds us and saves us." He pointed to the circle where the Tribe sat. "The circle is the earth that nurtures and keeps us." He pointed to the leaves. "The many-colored leaves are the spirit of our ancestors." He put the end of the stick into the fire. "The fire is the fire of humanity that glows in our hearts."

He pulled out the stick. Again, it glowed brightly. Walking inside the circle, he stopped in front of each person, drawing a circle before each, as one after another they called out their names. There was an empty place for Rhae.

Again, he pushed the stick into the fire, then pulled it out, flaming. He walked outside the circle. As the fire passed over their heads, each said, "I am here."

"I am here," Klena repeated.

He sat down on the rug and smothered the fire on the stick with dirt. "We are the only ones left," he said.

"We are the only ones left," said the Tribe.

"We are the only survivors."

"We are the only survivors."

"We are the Survivors," Klena said loudly.

"We are the Survivors," the Survivors shouted back.

"But," Klena said softly, rubbing his scar, "we are the victims, too. For as long as we are willing to remember, we will be the victims, too. We must never forget what happened. Tonight, we honor those who died. Tonight, we honor all the victims of the Devastation. For we, too, are victims of the Devastation. What happened will be retold tonight. Those who died will be remembered tonight. Those who lived will be revived tonight. Tonight, we will die with the dead and we will live with the living. We will sing songs for the dead. We will sing songs for the living. We will dance for the earth that keeps us and for the earth that keeps the ashes of our ancestors. We will listen to the wind that cools our anger and the wind that warms the spirits of our ancestors. We will curse those who caused the Devastation and we will praise nature for letting us survive. Tonight, we remember. Tonight, we perform our duties for the dead and renew our bonds with the living. Tonight is the Ceremony. Now, the Ceremony begins."

Through the dark night, Klena looked at the fire. "The fire is floating up and tumbling down. It is grabbing the wood. The fire smokes and burns. Blue is the second age of fire."

He shook his head and murmured to himself, "Because they did not tend their fires, we are here."

He looked around at the faces of the Survivors and said, "It is impossible to tell what truly happened. There are no words for it. I will tell our meager story poorly. I do not know what to call it."

Thick clouds slid over the dark orange full moon above the eastern horizon. The Ground darkened. Klena watched the fire. Sitting cross-legged on the rug, he wrapped the bearskin around himself. He looked into the fire. Rocking slowly, the fire brightened and darkened his face. He relaxed as he stared into the fire. His eyes did not see what others saw, nor could they see what he saw. His breathing slowed and grew deep. Even the fire seemed to hush, waiting. In a soft voice, barely heard, Klena said, "The sun is warm for this time of year. A green day turns brown as they do at this time of year. People are busily doing what they usually do."

He stopped for a moment and took a deep breath. Everything was silent. "The world explodes!" he screamed.

"The ground rumbles." He jumped to his knees.

"The sky thunders." He thrust his arms into the air.

"The fire jumps from the ground." His clenched fists opened.

"The fire touches the sky. The sun glows angry red. The wind burns." He threw off his robe.

"Hot winds blow. Trees crash down. Homes crumble."

He crawled toward the fire throwing in handfuls and handfuls of leaves. "The ground throws black smoke."

The fire choked, then burst into roaring flames.

"The earth is afire!"

He turned from the fire. "The people are stunned. They walk as if dreaming. Charred skeletons walk aimlessly."

He grabbed his bowl and jumped to his feet. Stirring the clay, he took handfuls of it, smearing himself as he walked around the circle. "What were faces are no more." Klena poured clay over the heads of the Survivors.

He stared wildly at the Survivors. "Eyes, empty eyes, eyes filled with disillusion and helplessness, lifeless eyes, tugging silently from naked bodies, stare up from the ground."

He ran toward the fire, pointing into it, screaming, "I can see them, I can see them."

Their robes thrown to the ground, the naked Survivors poured clay from their bowls over themselves and crawled toward the fire, throwing in leaves, yelling, "I can see them."

Klena ran to the east and screamed into the darkness, "The Devastation!"

"I can see them." The mud dried on their faces. Deep cracks slashed through the clay. Their faces stiffened. Their hair singed. Steam rose from them. Sweat poured down them, mixing with the clay, drying into dark scars. "I can see them." They crawled closer to the searing fire. The light blinded them. Their faces defaced, still they yelled, "I can see them."

Klena thrust his arms toward the south and screamed into the darkness. "The Devastation!"

Some jumped to their feet and walked around the circle. Their arms hung down at their sides. They dragged themselves around the circle. Little swirls of dust followed their feet. The fire made them look inhuman. They looked like ghosts. Still they yelled, "I can see them."

Klena opened his clenched fists toward the west and screamed into the darkness, "The Devastation!"

Some pounded the ground with their fists. Their fists slammed on the ground together. Their shouts vanished in the fire. They moaned. They cried. They rolled in the dirt. Still they yelled, "I can see them."

Klena stretched his arms toward the north and screamed into the darkness, "The Devastation!"

A branch exploded. Klena whirled toward the fire. "The fire spreads. See the thick black smoke dirtying the sky. Feel the heat of burning lives. Smell the stench of burning deaths. Touch the ashes raining down, thick, black, hard, hot, stinging. Hear the crying. See the people. See their skin melting like burnt bark. See their limbs broken like dead twigs. See them bleeding, bleeding, bleeding. I shut my eyes, I can still see them. I can see them. The hurt, the burnt, cry for water."

"There is no water," yelled the Survivors.

"The hungry, the starving cry for food."

"There is no food."

"The diseased, the exhausted cry for rest."

"There is no rest."

"The maimed, the dying cry for death."

"Death takes them all."

Klena fell to his knees. He held his hands against his chest and cried, "The burnt, the starving, the exhausted cry for help. They cry for their mothers and fathers. They cry for their families. They cry for their friends. No one comes. The silent voices of the dead cry for help. They are not heard. No one comes to help.

"Oh!" Klena crawled toward the fire. "The fire reaches the heart of the wood." He clutched his chest, his fingers digging into his flesh. "The fire burns deeply. Red is the third age of fire."

He struggled to his knees and cried, "Tears fell on charred cheeks. Children never saw their parents again. Parents never saw their children again. Families never saw their families again. Friends never saw their friends ever again."

Klena moaned, "The animals that people raised died with the people that cared for them."

"The wild animals, blinded, starved and died," wailed the Survivors.

Klena moaned, "The plants that people raised died without the people that cared for them."

"The wild plants burnt to their roots and died," wailed the Survivors.

Klena wept as he went on. "My parents are dead. My brothers are dead. My sisters are dead. My friends are dead. I am alone. I feel weak, and so lonely. Everything I lived for is dead. I do not know if I will live or die. I do not care. I am sick. Everything I remember makes me sick. Everything I eat makes me sicker. Everything tastes like death. I cannot digest anything. My stomach always aches. I vomit. Do you see the purple blotches on my face? They are all over my body. Do you see them? I have no hair either. All my hair fell out. I am afraid to touch myself. I am afraid of what is inside of me. Have I told you that my mouth bleeds? Do you know that I cannot control myself. Yes, I dirty myself. Am I making you sick? I am sick of it, all of it. I want to tell everyone, but there is no one. If I die perhaps it will stop. But I have no hope for death either. I have seen too much of it."

The flames flickered in his eyes as he stared deeply into the fire. "I have seen too much of it. I have no dreams. I have no hopes. I am tired of trying to make sense out of it. It would be worse if I could make sense out of it. But I do not care. I feel nothing. All the blood inside me flows slowly cold. Living does not interest me anymore. My mind is blank. My heart is tired. I hide in myself and cower. 'I do not see the dead.' I say to myself. 'Death has not taken over,' I say to myself, 'for I am yet alive.' Dying looks so simple. If death could just take me like it took the others, dying would be simple. If I do not have to do it myself. I do not even want death. I am tired of feeling nothing. Feeling nothing is death, too. I am tired of death. I must find food.

"Food! It is food I dream about when I fall asleep. It is food I think about when I wake up hungry. It is food that drives me to stagger naked through the ruins. Look, a weed, a living weed! 'Can I eat it?' It tastes horrible, but I do not spit it out. I chew it and chew it until it tastes like a feast. It tastes like sand, but I swallow it. I must find another of those weeds. It is food.

"Today, I must find something to eat. Tomorrow, I must find something to eat, again. Winter is here. Nothing can be done for the dead rotting on the ground. They will not need their clothes this winter. I have found a hut to shelter me. This hut will not help me if there are more explosions. But there are no more explosions. The sky is quiet. The snow is falling over the dead.

"The dead still lie on the ground. Around them, all they had built lies dead on the ground. The snow falls. The burnt buildings fall. The snow falls. The dead trees fall. The snow covers the naked mountains. The snow covers the broken valleys. It is the snowiest, coldest winter ever, since ever starts now. The ice freezes thickly over the flowing rivers. The clouds come and go and come and go. The sun goes and comes back. It is a clear day. I feel a warm breeze. Soon, the ice breaks loudly. Spring is here. Soon, the rivers carry the ice away. Spring is here. I am here. Green grass and young trees grow from among the skeletons on the ground, from where the dead still lie on the ground. The dead have become the new earth.

"What? What do you ask? It is the fire. It is still grasping the wood, and crackling. The fire burns clearly. Bright is the fourth age of fire.

"Who will ask the question?" asked Klena.

Jamu stood and walked behind the Survivors until he stood opposite Klena, with the fire between them. He turned toward Klena and through the loud crackling of the fire, shouted, "Why—" He stopped and scratched his head and looked around the circle as he fidgeted from foot to foot. He shouted again, "Why—" He paused for a long while, then shrugged his shoulders and said, "I forgot the question."

"That is all right," Klena said, smiling at Jamu. "This is your first time asking the question. It has been forgotten before by the youngest Survivor. Next year, Jamu, you will remember. Why did we survive when so many died?"

Jamu shouted, "Why did we survive when so many died?" He walked proudly back to his place in the circle and sat down.

Rubbing the dried clay off his scar, Klena said, "Many died in the explosions. Some, who did not die in the explosions, died in the fires. Some, who did not die in the fires, died of thirst. Some, who did not die of thirst, died of hunger. Some, who did not die of hunger, died of exhaustion. Some, who did not die of exhaustion, died of despair. Some who died had forgotten how to live. Some died by their own hands. Some died before they learned how to live. Some newborns died of disease. Some died before they were born. Many died of the

Sickness. Many died, but we survived. Why did we survive when so many died?

"We do not know the answer." Klena shook his head. "Many died without ever knowing why the Devastation happened. Without ever knowing why it happened, we survived. Yes, we survived. In a world filled with fear, we survived. In a world filled and buried by death, we survived. In a world where everything we knew and trusted and believed died, we survived. In a world where everything we loved died, we survived. The ones who tried to silence everyone but themselves failed. We are the Survivors and we will never forget or stay silent." Klena shouted, "We may never know why—"

"We are here," they shouted together.

Klena shouted louder, "But we will live without knowing why—"

"We are here."

"And we will continue to live without knowing why—"

"We are here."

Klena covered his face as he rocked back and forth. His voice sounded far away. "For a while, those who lived feared everything. For everything will never be the same again. For a while, those who lived feared nothing. For nothing will ever be the same again. Still those who live fear for their lives. For the Sickness has been in our midst ever since."

Klena clutched his head. His face paled. His eyes darted fearfully. His voice quivered. "Still, they die. They fight for food. They steal. Still, they die. We are alone. The winds blow, the warm winds of summer, the gentle breezes of childhood, and the winds take the children of the Devastation, the Survivors, away."

"We are here."

Klena stared into the fire. "Listen! The fire is both crying and laughing. It is singing and dancing. The fire dances in clouds of singing sparks. Many colors is the fifth age of fire."

Klena stood and stepped toward the fire. "We are judged forever both by our lives and by our deaths."

Pointing to the sparks floating into the darkness, he shouted, "Who judged how our ancestors lived their lives and who sentenced them to death? Who judged those who lived before the Devastation?" He walked around the circle. "They were like us," he said, "they ate and slept, worked and played, built homes and raised children, laughed and cried, loved and hated."

He stopped on the rug. Staring into the fire and up at the sparks, he shouted, "Who judged those who died in the Devastation? They died helplessly. They died horribly. They died inhumanely. Judges, of what were they guilty?"

The Survivors stood and held hands as Klena continued, "The scars of the Devastation will be remembered. These wounds that humans have given to humans will not heal, not in one or two generations."

"Not in one or two generations," repeated the Survivors.

"These pains that humans have dealt to humans will not fade, not in ten or twenty generations."

"Not in ten or twenty generations."

"These miseries that humans have handed down to humans will not disappear, not in one hundred or two hundred generations."

"Not in one hundred or two hundred generations."

"The dead of the Devastation will be remembered and recounted for all the generations of humanity."

"For all the generations of humanity."

Klena shouted loudly and scornfully, "We, the Survivors, deny the leaders, the murderers, what they sought most. We will not honor those who killed so many. We do not care about their fame. We do not care about their glory. We do not care about their victory. There are no reasons convincing enough. May they have been cursed to the end of their days. May their spirits have been buried by the bones of their victims. May they never be remembered. Their horrid deeds live on, but their names will be forgotten forever, banished from our memories as if these murderers were never born, never lived, never dishonored their names and the names of their families and the names of their friends and the names of their fellow humans. These leaders, seekers of fame and glory and victory, could not see beyond themselves. They cared only for themselves and not for the lives of their people and the children of their people and the children of their children. They cared only for their names and their desire to be remembered. The leaders who caused the Devastation have left no names worth remembering. We, their victims, strike them from our memories. We shut them out of our lives forever."

"We shut them out of our lives forever," said the Survivors.

Klena turned away from the fire. The cold north wind blew sharply against his face. He stretched his arms out into the darkness and said, "None of us are invulnerable to death. But there is that death that we can welcome, peaceful death that comes gently with the fullness of age. And there is that other death, violent death that pulls us away from our lives, rips us away from our families, tears us away from our friends, too soon."

The wind died as he stepped off the rug into the darkness, imploring, "We ask not for immortality. We ask only for death that is like the kind touch of an old love welcoming us back into the soft bosom of the earth. We ask that all should be able to die this way. We ask that all should be able to die in peace."

Klena turned and fell to his knees. He stretched out his arms and opened his hands toward the fire. He looked forlornly into the fire. His eyes filled with tears. His voice trembled. "I cannot tell the stories you told. I do not remember the words. I cannot sing the songs you sung. I do not remember the music. I cannot see what you saw. I cannot hear what you heard. I cannot feel what you felt. I want to talk to you, but I cannot remember your voice. I want to laugh with you, but I cannot remember your smile. I want to touch you, but your touch has faded from my skin. I cannot remember our hands together. I cannot remember our arms around each other. I cannot remember you holding me or me holding you. I cannot touch your face. I cannot kiss your lips. I cannot remember you," he cried, "I cannot remember."

Klena stood and lamented, "Always we try to remember. Always we try to retell. Always we try to revive. Words are an awful failure for us. We cannot feel the lost spirits of those who died. We cannot touch the lost spirits of those who died. We cannot hear the lost spirits of those who died. Words are an awful failure for them. Those who died are separated from us always. Those who died are gone from us always. Those who died are parted from us always. Words are an awful failure for us all."

Hands reached out for outstretched hands. Arms pulled bodies close as they hugged, then parted. Hearts pounded as feet pounded the hard ground. Feet slapped the ground hard and fast. Dust rose and stuck to hands slapping moving thighs. Hands clapped loudly. Heads bobbed. Shoulders swayed. Hips shook. Wild feet danced and danced.

Songs were sung and sung again, songs with words without meanings. They were sung loudly, for being alive with other singing, living beings. Voices and hearts sung with joy. Faces glowed with life in the light of the dying fire.

Bent arm whirled around bent arm as Jascha and Broda danced together. They sung, "We are here." Krilu spun as he jumped over the fire, then back again, his feet closer to the hot coals. Traro picked up his daughter, threw her high in the air, and caught her as she came down. He roared. She laughed. After Traro safely handed the girl to her, Mre grinned, too. Mekla and Sra hugged and kissed as they danced, their sons dashed around the circle. Tya sprung into the air and Clata caught her in his arms. Jamu and the youngest girl shook their bottoms from side to side, while Klena stood behind them, clapping his hands above his head. Hsoro danced into the darkness and only his singing was heard until he reappeared at the other side of the circle and whirled Ruu around in his arms. They sang together, "We are here."

The wind sang through the forest as the moon hugged the treetops to the west. Broda helped Jascha down, then flopped down himself. Jascha laughed as Broda panted loudly. The singing subsided and the dancing slowed as the Survivors, winded and exhausted, danced until they fell or lay down, wiping the sweat off themselves, breathing hard into the cold air. The children danced and sang the longest, but even they eventually slowed and stopped and sat down.

"Ah," Klena said. "Resting on the wood, the fire burns hot. Dark is the sixth age of fire."

He turned to his right and carefully opened a purple velvet pouch, delicately embroidered. Gently, he slipped off the pouch. He leaned over, picked up, and raised toward the fire a beautiful gold chalice. Golden lithe figures, worn down beyond recognition, seemed to dance on the chalice as the glimmering fire reflected darkly on it.

He picked up the clay pitcher and poured water into the chalice. Klena walked around the circle. In front of each Survivor, he lowered the chalice to waiting lips. Each took a sip, then said, "I am here."

Klena raised the chalice to his lips, took the last sip, then said, "I am here." He sat down and slid the chalice back into its pouch. He turned to the Survivors and asked, "Who stands for their dead?"

"I stand," said Ruu, "for my mother, Rhae."

Klena stood. He held the carefully prepared birch stick. With great patience and love, he had shaved many long fine curls into the wood until they covered the stick. He walked to Ruu and handed her the stick.

Ruu stood in the empty place for Rhae. Holding the stick gently in her hands, she turned to the fire and said, "For the recent death of my mother, Rhae, we sacrifice this wood. We give you this humble flame. May it give you light and warmth. May you rest in peace." Ruu laid the stick in the fire.

The stick blazed as Klena said, "Those who are dead are dead. They are beyond us. The dead are with the dead. We are with the living. We live, but with sadness that never goes away."

Klena knelt by the fire, picked up a handful of cool ashes, and said, "We live in the ashes of our ancestors. Their bones are in the dirt. Their spirits are in the wind. The ashes of our ancestors touch us when we feel the dirt under us, when we feel the ashes on us." He spread the ashes over himself. "In the ashes, they are here."

The Survivors picked up handfuls of ashes, spread them over themselves, and said, "In the ashes, they are here."

The oak tree and the village, the pond and the valley, the forest and the mountains, all that felt familiar to them, all that the Survivors loved so dearly, all that they knew and trusted, took form and grew out of the darkness as the night waned and another morning approached.

"Feel it! The fire is revived again, stirred and awakened by the breeze of a new morning. The fire glows. All colors is the seventh age of fire."

Klena rose to his knees. His voice sounded strained and tired. "No one came to help. No hero helped us. No messiah helped us. No God helped us. Nature helped us because we did not die. She cared for us and tended us as we healed. She comforted and nurtured us as we grew. Her bounty grew back and we survived. Nature is our true family and friend. We have no need for the Old God. In our moment of desperate need, the Old God abandoned us. He did not feed us, he did not clothe us, he did not shelter us. He did not love us. We owe nothing to the Old God. We have no need for the Old God. How can we believe in a deathless God when there have been so many deaths? How can we believe in a God that does not understand what it is to die? How can a deathless God ever understand what it is to have death so close that you do not know if you are already dead? Listen to me, Old God, I, Klena, shaman of the Survivors, will tell you about death and life. It is in life that we needed you, and you did not help. We need you here and now, and you have not helped. If you demand death as a reward for life, then what are we to believe life is for? If life is a punishment, then what is our reward for not dying?"

Looking into the coals, Klena rocked back and forth, and in a weary voice said, "He, and all he wanted us to believe, did not survive the Devastation. The Old God is no more. He did not want to stop it, or he did not care to stop it, or he could not stop it, but he is no more. He left us to survive, or he forgot us, or we did not matter to him. No matter, he is no more. And we are here."

"We are here," repeated the Survivors.

"This was the way of the Old God. He answered prayers or did not as it satisfied him. He made hunger, poverty, disease, and war as it satisfied him. He made happiness, joy, love, and peace as it satisfied him. But the people lost faith in his way, no matter what they wanted to believe. No matter, he is no more. And we are here."

"We are here," said the Survivors.

"We are alone," said Klena.

"We are alone."

"The Old God is gone."

"We are alone."

"No heroes will help us."

"We are alone."

"No saviors will save us."

"We are alone."

"We will survive."

"We are alone."

"We are here," said Klena.

"We are here," said the Survivors.

"We are here!" shouted Klena.

"We are here!" shouted the Survivors.

Overhead, in the oak tree, the bluejays awoke first, as always, and loudly, as always, as the silent gray dawn lightened the world.

Klena stood and looked around. Quietly, he said, "The long night is ended. We have lived to another day. Our story is ended, but it lives always inside us. We have lived a lifetime tonight. We have lived a lifetime of the people called the Survivors. We, the Survivors, are here to tell this story. Remembering this story and telling it to our children is our responsibility. Our children will remember and tell it to their children for that is their responsibility. Every generation will remember and every year they will tell this story because the Devastation did not happen just long ago, but, again, here, tonight, to us."

As Klena led the Survivors to Teardrop Pond, he said, "Everything has its end. Yet, our deeds live on. Our lives are for others to remember."

The Survivors, burnt, bruised, and scratched, scraggly, ash-covered, mud-caked, and naked, waded into the pond, scattering the thin gray mist, breaking the calm dark surface. Circles of waves skimmed across the water as they gathered in a circle, held their outstretched hands over their heads, looked to the east, and waited. Glowing bright gold, the sun rose peacefully over the horizon. They waited until it cleared the horizon, until the whole circle of it returned to the deep blue sky, until it gleamed through the bare trees, until its light shined brightly on them. They shouted together, "We are here!"

"We are here," their voices echoed throughout the valleys and mountains.

They cheered. They hugged and kissed. They laughed and splashed and patted each other until everyone dove into the cold water. Families washed families. Friends washed friends. Everyone helped each other until they had all washed themselves. Together, they waded to shore.

The Survivors, pale, small, and thin, tired, cold, clean, and naked, walked back to the village. They took their robes and bundled themselves against the morning chill. They waved and smiled to each other as they separated, returning to their huts. They crawled into their huts, and soon, fell asleep.

The world of the Survivors settled into silence.

Third Day

CHAPTER 24

Restlessly, barely under the edge of sleep, Hsoro dreamed. "I am walking, walking shakily. I feel dizzy, hungry, and tired. Every few steps I stumble. I grab onto trees. My hands are nothing but bones and pale flesh. Staggering, I keep walking. I must keep walking. I have been walking a long, long while. I do not know where I am. I do not know where I am going. I am scared. Everything feels strange. The ground is incredibly rocky and slippery. I slip nearly every step I take. My legs feel weak. My head hurts terribly. I look down and all around me lay bones, bare bones, a mountain of white bones, all pointing the same direction. They point to where I am walking. I try to turn away but I cannot. The path turns sharply up. The trees disappear. I can barely breathe but I keep climbing. I do not know how. I do not know why. I have no strength, none. I am covered by a cold, thick fog. I cannot see my feet. My feet cannot feel the ground. I hear laughter up ahead, loud, wild laughter. Suddenly, the fog disappears. I stop. I am startled. Here, in front of me, sits a huge golden chair, and sitting on it, a huge heavy man. His beard is long and white. He wears a long white robe. In his left hand, he holds a golden rod with a globe on top. At his right arm sits a young man with wide brown eyes, brown curly hair, and a curly sparse beard. He sits calmly smoothing the unkempt hair of the old man. The old man is laughing merrily. His belly shakes his robe. He leans over, picks up something, and lays it on the arm of the throne. Taking his scepter, he kills the struggling thing. He takes the limp thing and drops it into his mouth, then pulls it out and tosses it away. Hovering white beings fly to the thing and swarm over it. From the mouth of the smiling white man, blood drips down. He leans over and stares at me with bloodshot eyes. He laughs loudly and bellows, 'Ah, there are more of them. They survive. I knew I created a smart stock this time. Come, my child, you are next!' "

Hsoro awoke screaming. He jumped up, gasping. His heart

pounded. His body shivered. Sweat dripped down his face. He buried his face in his trembling hands.

Ruu grabbed him and pulled him close to her. She held him tightly and rocked him in her arms, whispering over and over, "It is all right now."

He began to breathe more deeply, calmly. He shivered less. He shook his head and pushed Ruu away. He stuck his head out of the hut.

"What is wrong?" she asked.

All the Survivors stopped and stared at the wild-eyed look of Hsoro.

Hsoro yelled, "Traro, come quickly!"

He pulled his head back into the hut and knelt. He looked deathly pale.

Ruu covered him with his hide. "What is wrong?"

"You will find out soon enough."

"Tell me now. What is wrong?"

"Hsoro."

"Come in, Traro, quickly."

"Are you all right?" Traro asked as he crawled in. He crossed his legs and began to sit.

The hide covering Hsoro dropped to the ground as he grabbed Traro hard with both hands. He pulled himself close to Traro. Their faces nearly touched. "Traro, what if it is—" His voice cracked. He took a deep breath. "What if it is the Old God?"

"What if what is the Old God?" interrupted Ruu.

"Traro, what if it is the Old God?"

"Calm down, Hsoro." Traro laid his hands gently on the shoulders of his friend. "Calm down. We do not know what it is."

"What what is?" Ruu interrupted loudly.

Traro and Hsoro looked at her. Both men looked worried.

"What what is?" repeated Ruu more loudly.

The men turned to each other, their hands on the shoulders of the other. They looked into the eyes of each other. Neither spoke. Each waited for the other to speak, for the other to find the words. Traro broke the silence. "There may be something in the Cave."

"There is something in the Cave," Hsoro said, "or someone."

"We do not know what it is," said Traro quietly.

Ruu leaned toward the men. Her voice, now quieter, sounded worried. "Is it still in the Cave?"

Traro turned toward her. "Maybe."

Hsoro shrugged his shoulders. "We do not know."

"It may be gone." Traro tried to force a smile.

Again, Hsoro shrugged his shoulders. "We do not know."

Ruu leaned closer to the men. She lowered her voice and whispered, "Should we tell the others?"

"What can we tell them?" Traro whispered. "There is nothing we can tell them. We do not know what it is and we do not know if it is still there. We do not know if it has hurt us, or if it wants to hurt us, or if we want to hurt it." He straightened his back and pulled his hands into fists. "This I do know." His voice sounded stronger, more confident. "This is my home, our home, our only home, and my family will not be afraid in their own home."

"Tell no one," Hsoro said. "There is no reason to tell them what we do not know and we do not know enough to tell them anything."

Ruu tried to sound calm but her voice trembled slightly when she asked, "What do we do?"

"Nothing," answered Traro.

"Watch," answered Hsoro. "Watch, be patient, and be careful."

Traro nodded and began to rise. "You rest, Hsoro. I will guard downstream, but only for today. There is more important work to do than wait for something that may never come. Here, there is a hungry tribe and we have hunting we must do."

Hsoro nodded in agreement. "This evening I will watch and that will be all. Tonight, we hunt. Be careful, Traro."

"I am not afraid." He turned and crawled out.

Ruu waited until she heard Traro walk away. She turned and faced Hsoro. She looked worried and tense. Her eyes stared into his. She did not speak for a long while. Finally, in a barely controlled voice, she asked, "Did it kill Rhae?"

His eyes left hers and looked down. He covered his face with his hands and shook his head. "I do not know."

"What did kill Rhae?" she asked.

Hsoro looked up. His eyes seemed to plead for an answer. He lowered his face and shook his head again. "I do not know."

"The others will ask. What should we tell them?"

"I do not know." His voice sounded strained. "I do not know. Tell them I do not know. Or tell them nothing. Death comes suddenly sometimes, we do not know why. If they need to hear something, tell them we do not know of the ways of death. Tell them I know nothing."

"Are you afraid?"

"No." He grabbed both her hands. He held them tightly. He stared into her eyes. "No, I am not afraid of death."

His grip softened until his hands hung loosely in hers. He took a deep breath. His chin dropped to his chest. His face sank into its own shadows. "I am so tired." He took another deep breath. "There is much to do, so much to do."

He wrapped himself in his hide and crawled to the doorway. He paused and Ruu heard him quietly say, "We must not be afraid of life."

He crawled out.

CHAPTER 25

The sun gave little light and no warmth. Only pale light seeped through the clouds. From the west, the clouds had tumbled in. Thick, heavy clouds, piling up fast, swallowed the sky. The wind pushed the clouds, stuffing them tightly from horizon to horizon. The sky had lost its color. It was full of similar shades of dark whites and light blacks crammed into a solid conglomerate of gray. All hung coolly overhead. The lighter clouds looked nearer but the darker clouds were often closer to the earth and the lighter ones farthest away from the busy workings of the Survivors.

Broda waded across Walking Stream. The cold, rushing water flowed around his leg, under his stump, and passed his crutch. He dug his crutch and foot into the mud of the far shore and pulled himself up. Water dripped off him as he walked away. He carried only a knife, some twine, and a pouch, half-filled with meat and nuts, hanging from his belt.

A mouse nervously gnawed a seed. A meadow vole picked up a piece of bark and darted toward the stream. With a nut in its mouth, a chipmunk ran ahead on the path. A small brown bird, a creeper, crept up a maple tree in spirals, digging out insects with its curved beak. Scarlet leaves fluttered down around Broda as a red squirrel jumped to a branch, scampered up the maple tree, and across another branch. A hungry marten chased it. They raced into the forest. The branches shook, and then, lay still. Broda walked on. His work awaited him.

Stopping occasionally, he leaned against his crutch and looked through the underbrush. To the side of the path lay a narrow run. Along it, heavy rocks stood gaping with their ends held up precariously with thin, small sticks. Underneath the rocks lay tempting twigs with nuts and meat. Broda examined each deadfall as he walked down the path.

As a father knows each of his children, Broda knew each of his deadfalls, and its quirks. This one, until lately, seemed happy, falling properly and often. The next one seemed dull, its bait never touched. The one next to that seemed edgy, dropping often without anything underneath. Broda knelt beside another deadfall, the stubborn one.

"A rock and a stick," he grumbled, "yet you would not fall if a moose came through here, no less a mouse." The bait under it had been eaten, so too, the grass under the bait, even the pried stick had been chewed, but still, the rock stood. Broda opened the pouch on his belt. He took out some fresh nuts and meat, put them on the end of his crutch, and slid them under the stubborn deadfall.

Today, as for so many days lately, he stayed on the path and kept walking. So his scent would not scare away the animals, he avoided the run. He shook his head and sighed as he kept seeing empty deadfalls.

Early in the spring, usually before Walking Stream had slid fully back between its banks and the mud around it had dried, Broda crawled through the bushes and vines building deadfalls and snares. He set up many immediately to catch the bleary-eyed, skinny, hungry hibernators as they hurried to fill their bellies. By then, the skinny, hungry Survivors, and Broda with his hearty appetite in particular, were in desperate need of fresh meat, no matter how little. The animals used these same runs year after year, and throughout the snowless seasons, the traps stayed in them. A few stayed unset in the runs throughout the spring and into the summer, until they almost disappeared into the forest. When the animals avoided the old traps, he set the new ones. By autumn, especially late in autumn with the cold grip of winter clawing at his ribs, Broda set every deadfall and snare. At the first snow, when the tribe left for the Cave, Broda checked all the traps, then triggered them. Nothing would be caught that would not be eaten.

A proud and practiced hunter, Broda walked this path every day now, checking. He would let no animals suffer. Also, he knew that a dead animal would be stolen. Not all creatures hunted honestly. Some creatures merely took.

Broda stopped. Ahead, a young sapling stood upright, too upright. Shaking his head, Broda walked toward it. He leaned against his crutch and glared at the empty noose on the ground. He looked up the trunk of the sapling. Near its top, where it should be, the twine was gone. He stamped his crutch on the ground. "Damn dumb animal! You must have gone for quite a ride when that tree sprung. Maybe you learned something. I bring you good food and you eat twine. Why do you think I bring you good food? Do not think about that. Why not eat the bait I bring you and go for the ride I planned? Damn dumb animal!"

He took out his knife and cut a fresh notch farther up the trunk of the sapling. "It is only a tiny cut, little tree. I know it hurts, but you will heal quickly. You are still young."

He tied a fresh length of twine into the notch. From the ground, he picked up a carved piece of pine and cut the piece of twine off it. "Listen to me, little wood, you must be quiet. The animals are skittish in the autumn, so do not scare them. If you sit still and stay quiet, they will trigger you easily."

The free end of the twine that hung from the top of the sapling, he tied to the block of wood. He took a handful of dirt and rubbed it over the twine. As he strained to pull down the top of the sapling, he groaned, "Your bark is tougher than my old skin. Come on, little tree, bend! This will not hurt you, I promise. You will live a long, long time and forget that I bent you. Soon you will be big and strong and will laugh at the next man who tries to bend you. But now, bend! Please, as a favor for an old man!"

Broda fell hard on his back, but his strong hands firmly held the top of the sapling. With his foot, he pushed the piece of wood against a wooden spike driven deep into the ground. Slowly, he let the sapling up. His foot maneuvered the wood as it slid up the spike and caught against a carved notch. The taut twine vibrated. The snare held.

He sat on the ground. With another piece of twine, he tied a slip knot while he grumbled, "Look at yourself, old hunter. You have lived a long life in the forest and still you are dumber than the animals. Have you learned nothing? They will not come near a fresh snare, it reeks of human."

As he tied the other end of the twine to the piece of wood, his stomach growled loudly. "Shh! Your damn roaring will scare away all the animals. I know you are hungry, but that is no reason to shake the whole forest."

He pushed two twigs into the ground on opposite sides of the run. Between the two twigs, he hung the noose. He tightened the noose around his fist. Laying his hand flat on the ground, he lowered the bottom of the noose until it brushed the top of his hand. "I can hear them laughing at me," he muttered as he adjusted the snare, "lying on their fat bellies, resting in their snug, warm burrows. They can rest, they are ready for winter. I must keep working. An empty stomach knows no rest."

He scattered dirt and leaves around the snare so it blended into the forest. Laying twigs on both sides of the run, he narrowed it so the animals could only get through by triggering the snare. He moved a single leaf from one side to the other and gently laid a small twig beside it. He placed stones in a line on the other side. He fussed over dead leaves, dried twigs, and plain stones. When, at last, everything looked good to him, he nodded slightly. He did not smile. He knelt on the path, leaned against his crutch, and gazed deeply into the forest.

"What is wrong? Are you unhappy with me? Are we no longer friends? What did I do wrong? It is not my fault that I must kill. Hunting is what I must do, you know that. I take only what you give me. I must kill to eat. Is that wrong?"

He walked slowly down the path, checking his traps. Every one was empty. His eyes looked tired. His chin dropped to his chest. His shoulders sagged. He shook his downcast head and whispered, "You can hear me. You know what I have to say. I am a crippled old man. For me, it does not matter. But for the tribe, please, I cannot face them with another day of failure. I would rather die here than go back empty-handed."

Broda stopped. The forest seemed to pause, and ponder. The old hunter and the old forest stood together. From the stillness of the forest came a tiny shriek. Against the trunk of a pine tree leaned a small pole. From the pole hung a noose. From it, a struggling squirrel swung by its neck. Broda slit its throat.

He leaned against his crutch and sighed, "So you still want me to live. It is just another mouth for you to feed. But, you know all the mouths that you must feed and what you must do to feed them. You are a wise, old hunter, and an old friend. Thank you."

He tied the squirrel to his belt and walked home.

CHAPTER 26

Deep in the forest, a large black rodent shuffled through the thick underbrush. Staying hidden in the shadows, she crawled under decaying trees and through low passages between rocks. Her squat body, filled with fat for the coming winter, swayed clumsily from side to side. The stiff, pointy quills on her back shook as her sharp claws rooted through the fallen leaves in search of salt. A branch fell on her head. She lifted her head and looked up quizzically at the skinny man standing over her. Hsoro brought the branch down again. Blood spurted from the head of the porcupine as she slumped and slowly rolled on her side.

Into the cold, rushing water of Walking Stream waded Krilu. Swaggering, he kicked through the water. His foot slipped on the bottom and he drove the end of his spear into the stream bed and leaned hard against it, steadying himself. He carried his spear on his shoulder as he again splashed down the stream. His eyes searched from side to side. He pushed over piles of leaves and turned over rocks along the shore with the end of his spear. He shoved its point into holes at the edge of the water. Each time it came out clean and bloodless. Each time he scowled and turned to the other shore. The babbling stream and biting insects annoyed him. He smacked a fly on his neck and squeezed it between his fingers before dropping it into the water. He spit into the stream. As his impatience grew, he gripped his spear more tightly.

Above the waterline on the bank, he noticed a high mound of freshly cut pondweeds and cattail stalks. At the bottom of the mound lay a pile of gnawed cattails. He leaned over and poked the end of his spear into the mud of the stream bed until it slid into a hole. He pulled out his spear and stepped down. He felt the tunnel collapse under his foot. He blew into his hands, rubbed them together, then grabbed his spear. Up the bank, he crept. A strong musky scent filled the air. He stood over the mound and stared down at it. He smiled as he stabbed his spear hard into the heart of the mound. He thrust his spear in again and again, ripping the mound apart, tearing it down, mauling and scattering the nest widely around him. He rooted through the remains with his spear, but found no animal. Angrily, he kicked the rubble down the bank.

A small furry animal poked her head out of a hole down the bank, then dashed to the stream. Krilu heard the scurrying. He grabbed his spear and ran after her. The dark brown animal slid into the water. Krilu slipped on the mud and fell to his knees. He jumped up and sprinted after her again. His fiery eyes glared at the animal as he splashed through the water. She glided through the water, her thick fur glistening. Krilu slashed at her with his spear, but she swam easily out of reach.

Krilu stepped up on a dry rock protruding from the stream and jumped from rock to rock. The water grew faster and faster. The rocks grew more slippery and farther apart. He leapt to a low rock and stood panting nearly on top of her. He cocked his arm and threw. The spear stabbed into the water. The muskrat swam away unharmed.

He waved his arms wildly. His foot slipped off the rock. Krilu fell over backward into the stream with a loud splash. He sat dripping in the water and watched the muskrat swim calmly away and his spear float gently downstream.

"Damn you!" he snarled.

He slammed his fists furiously against the water, soaking himself more.

On the near side of Walking Stream, at the edge of the meadow, the bright gold leaves of an aspen tree shivered. Under it, sat Klena, wrapped in hides. He laid a handful of dried bark on the ground, then blew on a smoldering stick. He pushed the stick into the bark. Mekla brought an armful of green pine twigs and laid them beside his father. The bark began to smoke. A small flame flickered. Klena placed some dried leaves on the fire.

Mekla dressed himself in thick winter hides. Over his head, he pulled on a fur covering with small eyeholes cut into it. Around his neck, he hung a thong the length of his arm span with mittens tied to its ends. He unsheathed his knife and tucked it into the belt of his breeches.

Klena stripped the needles from the twigs. He put some of the twigs into the fire. They crackled, sputtered, and popped. A gray smoke rose from the fire. Klena sat and Mekla knelt under the tree while the smoke swelled into a growing, whirring cloud. Mekla nodded to his father, then began to climb.

He climbed up into the din of angry buzzing. All around him, the air felt thick with motion. Wrapped in heavy hides, he moved slowly like a sluggish bear. With the extra weight of the hides, the covering over his face, and the thick smoke, he could barely breathe. He stopped in a crotch of the tree to catch his breath. He reached under the covering and wiped the sweat from his face and the tears from his eyes. Klena put more twigs into the fire. A billowing cloud of smoke covered Mekla. He put on the mittens, then pulled the knife from his belt. Carefully, he climbed out on a branch. A storming mass of bees attacked him, but they could not get through the thick hides. The farther out on the branch he crawled, the more it swayed under his weight and the more the hive trembled. Klena dropped pine needles into the fire, smothering it, and sending up a dense puff of smoke. With the cloud of bees swarming over him and the cloud of smoke swirling around him, Mekla could hardly see. He felt a sting on his wrist. He lay flat on the branch and groped for the hive. His knife touched something. He hacked at the top of it. A bee landed inside his mitten, crawled up the back of his hand, and stung him. Mekla kept chopping at the bottom of the branch. He swung hard at it. He heard the hive plop on the ground. He tucked his knife back into his belt and slid over the side of the branch. While he dangled, a bee flew under his face covering and stung him on the neck.

"Ow!" He let go and fell to the ground. He rolled around on the ground, then jumped up, pulled off the face covering, and shook it out.

The air was full and loud of bees. Klena dumped a handful of dirt over the fire. He laughed while his son ran around, waving and shooing the bees. He walked over and patted him on the back. "You did well," he said, smiling. "How did they do?"

"Three stings, so far," said Mekla, rubbing his neck. "If I wasn't so sweet, they wouldn't like me so much."

"Come, we will get some mud on those stings."

"Oh no," Mekla grinned, his eyes sparkling, "not yet." He patted his stomach, jumped high in the air, and shouted, "Honey!"

Clata shivered as he stood on the shore of Teardrop Pond. The chilly water nipped at his bare toes. His feet ached in the cold mud. He stretched himself to his full height and pushed the blunt end of his spear into the mud. Slowly, the spear slid in. He pulled it out, walked a few strides, and stood over another small mound of mud. With his spear in front of him, held firmly with both hands, he again pushed the spear into the mud. The spear stopped. He pulled it up slightly, then pushed it down again. It tapped against something. He pulled up the spear, knelt on his knees, and dug into the mud. He uncovered a hard, dark shell. He dug around it until he could safely lift it from its hole. Picking up the sleeping turtle, he turned and carried it up the beach. He laid it on its back. The turtle still slept. Clata smiled proudly as he sat beside it. He rubbed the soles of his pale, numb feet. They felt only slightly better as he stood and hobbled down to the edge of the water. He took his spear and pushed it into another mound.

Scattered in the grassy field over the knoll from the village, five quiet children lay motionless on their bellies. Each child held a small wooden club and stared down a small hole. They lifted their heads and saw other shrugging shoulders, shaking heads, and serious faces. They checked once again their supply of stones. One child nodded to the others, picked up a stone, and dropped it into one of the holes. The children put their ears to the ground, gripped their clubs tightly, and waited. They heard nothing stirring underground. Raising their heads, they looked down into the darkness of each of their holes. Another child dropped another stone down a hole, and the children waited.

"Be careful, Tya!"

"Don't worry, Mother." Tya smiled as she pulled her blond hair away from the fire.

"Mothers always worry," said Sra.

Mre, sitting beside her, patting the acorn bread, nodded in agreement.

Sra, grinding acorns, looked up at her young daughter. The flickering fire made the bright eyes of Tya gleam and the fair skin of her face glow with a soft shade of pink. Sra asked, "Were we so pretty when we were young?"

Mre nodded.

"I was not pretty," Sra continued. "I always had too much work to do to care about how I looked. I cannot even remember if I cared how I looked."

"You cared," said Mre, smiling.

"Well, maybe."

Both sisters laughed.

"I saw you looking at yourself the other day," added Tya, giggling.

"Anyway," said Sra, "I can remember how hard we had to work."

"The work made us happy as children, it felt good to help," said Mre, staring into the fire. "We like to remember what makes us happy. I hope our children have happier times to remember."

"I hope their lives are easier—"

"—and they have time for more than work."

"Tya does," said Sra, smiling and looking up at her daughter, "she has time for Clata."

"Mother!" Tya stamped her foot hard on the ground. She felt embarrassed and could feel herself blushing. She turned to one of the forked, green poles pounded into the ground on opposite sides of the hearth. Browning over the fire between the poles was the hindquarter of the elk. She held it by its ankle and turned it.

Sra turned to Mre and said, "We worry when they are children and we worry when they are grown. When do we stop worrying?"

Mre shrugged her shoulders.

Sra looked up at Tya again. "Maybe when you are mated with Clata, I will worry less."

"Oh, Mother!" Tya could feel herself blushing again.

"When you are a mother, you will know what it is to worry."

"I will never worry!"

"That is what I said," the two sisters said in unison, then laughed.

Mre said, "Let us hope that they have fewer worries than we do."

The two women sat quietly, listening to the fire, watching the sparks rise and the meat cook.

"I miss Rhae," Sra said softly.

CHAPTER 27

The opening in the wall separated Ruu from the other women. She sat alone with her back to the village. She laid a leather bag in front of her and opened it. She took out a piece of rolled leather, unrolled it, and laid it out flat on the ground. From the bag, she took a granite cobble, a sandstone slab, an oaken club, a thick antler prong of an elk, a smaller elk prong, a tiny deer antler tine, a leather pad wrapped around the tooth of a wolf, and a small leather pouch. She arranged them on the right side of the leather mat. She turned the bag over. A large dark rock rolled out.

Ruu stared at the rock. Her hands felt cold and stiff. Cupping her hands around her mouth, she blew into them, and rubbed them together. She picked up the rock and inspected it. She turned it over and over, checking for flaws, while her hands slid over its surface, feeling its grain. She laid down the rock.

The granite cobble felt cold in the palm of her right hand. She held the hammerstone tightly. Leaning over, she tapped the rock with the hammerstone. She turned the rock and tapped again, turned it, tapped, turned it, and with every tap, the rock rang sharp and clear. Nodding her head, she put the hammerstone down, patted the turtle-shaped rock, and said, "Good flint."

She crossed her legs, picked up the rock, and held it against her thigh. With the hammerstone, she tapped the rock again. The rock shook on her thigh. Leaning closer, she struck it harder. A tiny sliver slipped off. She pushed the rock tightly against her thigh, bent nearer, and brought the hammerstone down again. Small chips of flint flew off. Turning the rock and hitting it repeatedly, she knocked off the protruding edges. She stopped and brushed off the rock. She put down the hammerstone and picked up the thick, blunted, elk antler prong. Precisely, and with less force, she poked off smaller chips. The rock shrank to roundness. Ruu picked up the rock and examined it. She put it back on her thigh. Punching chips from the top of the rock, she carved a ridge. She ran her hand over the finished ridge, then laid the antler punch down. With both hands, she picked up the rock. She checked the ridge, nodded, and laid the prepared core down in front of her.

She pushed back her hair and knelt over the rounded core. She turned the core, pointing the ridge to her right, and angled it, pointing it down and away from her. The sole of her foot she placed firmly on the core, steadying the rock. She picked up the smaller elk antler prong. The blunted tip of the prong she placed against the ridge of the core. She practiced twisting the punch. She picked up the oaken club and practiced swinging it at the punch. With the club in her left hand and the punch in her right, she bent over. Her weight held the rock down. She paused, took a deep breath and, with the club, hit the back of the punch. The tip of the punch jerked. The punch struck too far below the ridge. A flake fell off. It looked short and stubby. It left two ridges on the core. Gripping the punch and club tightly, she concentrated harder on the core. She knocked off one ridge, then the other. These blades were finer, but useless, too thick and with coarse edges. She grabbed all three and threw them over the wall.

Ruu glared at the rock. She put the core against her thigh and picked up the thick antler punch again. More slowly and carefully, she jabbed tiny slivers of flint off one side, turned the core around, and chipped away at the ridge from the other side, refining it. She laid the punch down and rubbed her hand over the ridge. It felt good and smooth. She lifted the core and looked across it. It looked straighter. She put the core down and stared at it, studying it. A badly prepared core would not yield long, sharp, useful blades.

Making stone blades, and the tools from them, was a long, tedious, thankless task. This would be her skill, Ruu had decided, and she worked hard at it. She persisted at it, forcing herself to go on, challenging and testing her will. It strained her patience and temper. She felt awkward at it. She disliked this work. Yet, she knew the importance of tools for the survival of the tribe. Without them, they were helpless. Each bad blade pained her.

Ruu leaned over the core again. She turned the core on its side and angled it away from her. She picked up the punch and club again and carefully lined up the punch to the ridge. She watched closely as the hammer hit the punch; a good blade slid off. She repeated each move; a blade crumpled onto the mat. Another blade crumpled from

the core, then a good blade slid off. Frustrations made her hate this
work. She knew it would go easier if she could make herself feel
calm, but Ruu did not feel calm. She forced herself to feel calm; a
blade cracked. She grew angrier; the only release for her anger was
the rock; she grew more frustrated.

She stood and brushed herself off. Blood trickled from a cut on her
right thumb. She wiped the blood off on her thigh. Her back and
shoulders felt tired and sore. Try as she might, she could never find a
comfortable working position. She rubbed and stretched her shoulders as she circled the rock, glowering at it as if it purposely withheld
its secrets from her. It seemed to fight her, and she fought it. The
rock sat there and did not tire nor anger nor bleed. Ruu sat over it
and chipped away at it again.

A broken blade fell on the mat. With rock, a mistake stayed a
mistake. The ruined blade lay there and seemed to mock her, "Millions of years to become this rock and you ruined me, you incompe-
tent fool, leave me alone." Another bad blade landed beside it, another cracked blade and a curse tore through the air. Ruu grabbed
the punch hard, placed its tip against the ridge, took a deep breath,
clenched her teeth, and smacked the punch with the club. A good
sharp blade slid easily off.

Blade by blade, the core shrank. Little by little, the work went on.
Ruu worked alone. She despised incompetence and felt embarrassed
by her own. The tribe appreciated her work, but she demanded
more. She judged herself harshly and only her own judgment mattered. She pushed herself to exhaustion, but the work always went
too slowly. A blade cracked as it came off. "Damn!" she yelled as she
threw the blade over the wall. "If only I could make these damn
blades half as sharp as my temper," she said while leaning over to
check a new blade. This one pleased her and she put it to her side.

Beside her, the pile of blades grew. Her back grew stiffer. Her
shoulders ached. Blood dripped from the fingertips of her calloused
hands. Dust stuck to her sweating face. Her head pounded from the
persistent pounding of the rock, and from hunger. Her stomach
growled. A blade dropped from the core. It looked thick and rough.
It felt heavy in her palm. She opened the small leather pouch and put
the blade inside. "It will make a good spear point, I will notch it
later." Between her knees, she held the core. She stared down at it,
then put the club and punch down. She turned to the pile of blades.

Each one, she picked up, inspected, and then arranged in size order from biggest to smallest. "Twenty," she said when she finished. She rolled the core back into the bag.

She picked up the biggest blade. The edges were so thin that they darkened when she held it in her hand. She picked up the small punch again. She chipped off the fragile point of the blade, making it shorter and thicker. It looked good. Against her hide-covered thigh, she scraped the blunted end. The scraper felt strong. She put it down and picked up the next blade. From good blades, scrapers are easy to make, and Ruu needed something easy to make. She felt tired and dizzy. She finished the second scraper. It looked strong enough to scrape off the flesh from the skin of a carcass before tanning it. The next scraper was harder to make, but when she finished it, she laid it beside the others and slid the three scrapers into a pile.

She pushed the sandstone slab in front of her and brushed off its flat top. She picked up a blade and laid it on the stone. With the punch, she chipped off one of its long, sharp edges. She picked up the blade and held it. Carefully along its edge, she tapped it with the punch, blunting the blade more. The other edge she kept sharp. Grinding it against the sandstone, she honed the edge finer. She laid it down on the mat, picked up the next blade, and repeated each step. The tribe used these blunt-backed knives for skinning carcasses, for butchering and carving meat, for notching bows before tying on the sinew strings, for notching shafts before attaching the stone arrow points, and for whittling sticks into sharp spears before fire-hardening their points. She inspected the new knife. It pleased her. She picked up the next blade, chipped off its edge, tapped it blunt, ground the sharp edge, checked the edge with her thumb, turned it over, ground the edge again, rubbed the grit off the knife on her thigh, and laid the finished knife down.

Ruu wiped the sweat from her face and neck, then rubbed her hand over the top of the sandstone. She spit on the stone. The next blade she honed its point and both its edges sharp. Set in a bone handle, this blade would make a fine stabbing knife. She examined it closely, then laid it beside the other three knives.

The next two blades were short and stout. She picked them both up and checked them, pressing her thumb against the duller of their points. One blade she laid beside the sandstone and the other she put on the stone. She grabbed the punch and bent over the blade. She knocked off its point. It broke at a good, sharp angle to its corner. She looked the blade over carefully. To turn a blade into a burin, a sturdy, sharp-pointed cutting tool used for chiseling bones and antlers into awls and needles, it took a strong yet precise hit. She lifted the end of the blade off the stone and lined up the corner and the antler punch. She hit it hard. The edge cracked cleanly the full length of the blade. The corner felt strong and sharp against her thumb. Ruu sighed in relief and wiped the sweat off her palms before picking up the next blade. It broke raggedly toward its corner. When hit, its edge crumbled. She cocked her arm to throw it over the wall, but brought it back down. She chipped the point blunt, then the edge flat, then ground it until the corner felt sharp. When she finished, she scowled at it and cocked her arm again, but laid it beside the other burin. It looked ugly to her, but usable.

Ruu stood and stretched her back and rubbed her neck. She looked down at the blades. "Eleven," she said, "eleven arrow points." She shook her head. She turned away, propped her elbows on the wall, and dropped her chin into her hands. Her hands ached. Her head felt heavy. She looked out over the browning meadow. Her mind wandered away to playful seasons, to scampering wildly through the golden meadow, to easy, giggly days of youth. She pushed against the wall as if trapped.

"Go on, I must go on," she muttered. "This work is boring and my life—" She slammed her hands hard against the wall. "Go on! Get back to work!" she shouted. She whirled and sat down.

She picked up the first blade and laid it on her lap. She stared at her strong hands. She breathed on them and rubbed the flesh together. She stretched her stiff fingers. On the mat, ten blades lay side by side like ancient fingers from the earth. Gnarled, the gray, stubby blades slanted to rough points.

She unwrapped the leather pad and laid the tooth of the wolf beside her. She put the pad in the palm of her left hand, placed the blade on the pad, and gripped the blade with her fingertips. The back of her hand she braced against her knee. She picked up the tiny deer antler tine. She placed its tip against the edge of the blade and pressed down and in against it. A tiny chip of flint fell from the underside of the blade.

Ruu detested this painstaking, nerve-wracking work, this slow, constant work. It demanded great patience and determination. These small, persistent, never-ending tasks bored her. They were dull, but necessary. The daily work of the women kept the Tribe well and nourished, but at the cost of long, uninspiring days.

She laid a new blade on the heel of her hand and maneuvered her fingers around the blade to lift its edge up slightly. With the tip of the flaker, blunted for better gripping, she chipped from the bottom of the blade. Chipping from the top of the blade, she still learned painfully, caused chipped fingernails and bloody fingertips.

Ruu longed for the excitement of the hunt. The hunt, too, was slow, arduous work. It demanded great patience and determination. This long, persistent, endless work was merciless. It was brutal, but necessary. It turned the lives of the men into cold, hungry lives of anticipation and frustration, of pain and cruel failure, and forced them face to face with death.

She held another new blade in her hand and leaned the weight of her body behind the flaker. By pushing hard but steadily against the bottom of the blade, the flake she wanted slid off. Sudden pushes caused mistakes, bad cuts on the blade, and on her hands. She pressed against the blade, giving the flaker a slight twist, and a flake came free.

The men, women, and children, each bore a share of the ceaseless work. Each was tied to the daily work of surviving. No one was free. There was no time for indolence or irresponsibility. For anyone retreating from the struggle, or wishing for escape, or lying idle, there was no place. The Tribe lived dependent upon nature, and she could, as she did this autumn for an unknown reason, withhold her bounty.

She laid the new arrow point on the mat. She put the flaker and pad down. Hunching over, she grabbed her aching stomach. She closed her eyes and rocked back and forth. Clenching her fists, she pounded her numb legs. She opened her eyes, then her fists. Bending over, she picked up the flaker and pad again. She looked at the blades and said, "Four more."

There was always work, always more work. The Survivors rarely had the luxury of rest. It was always a struggle, every year, every season, every day. They had no holidays. They could never leave their responsibilities. Life was stripped bare to its essence. Life itself was luxury.

She tapped the back of the blade flat. Gradually, she tapered its edges, honing them sharp, then diligently carved the tip. She touched the tip with her thumb and felt it press against her flesh. She picked up the tooth and, with it, notched the bottom corners of the triangular-shaped point. In the palm of her hand, she held the arrow point. It looked fine, almost delicate, and deadly.

With starvation near, the Survivors pushed themselves like hunted animals, their unseen predator always present, always stalking, waiting. Nature is unforgiving. Death is the punishment for mistakes.

She held the last arrow point in the palm of her hand and breathed a sigh of relief. She licked the edge of the point and leaned over the sandstone slab. She sharpened the point. The point shattered. She stared angrily at the crumbled pieces, shouted, and threw them away.

CHAPTER 28

Cold, tired, and hungry, the men straggled home from their hunting chores. Clata carried the awakening turtle, its stubby legs moving in search of its missing home. Hsoro held the dead porcupine. As he limped into the village, Broda cut the squirrel from his belt. Klena and Mekla, carrying wooden bowls filled with dripping honeycombs, laid them beside the hearth. Tya tasted the honey and smiled.

Gathered around the warming fire, the others noticed Krilu, squishing with every step, trying to walk quietly and unnoticed into the village. Seeing the angry scowl on his face, they said nothing.

With the small leather pouch lying beside her, Ruu sat with a pile of dark gray arrow points in front of her. On the sandstone, she ground a bright white piece of quartz. Krilu sat down and watched her. She kept her head down and concentrated on the sharp tip of the point. She rubbed it clean against her thigh, checked it, and sighed. Finished, she opened the small pouch and began sliding the points into it. Krilu reached out and took the white point. He closed his fist around it. He stood up and walked away. He did not thank her.

"When do we eat?" a hollow-sounding voice came from the hut of Kru.

Ruu put the pouch into the bag with the tools and tied the top closed.

"Soon," answered Sra.

"I am hungry now," she groaned.

Ruu threw the bag down and jumped to her feet. Her face reddened as she stomped toward the dingy hut. She clenched her fists and slammed them against the hut. A birch pole dropped off.

"You disgust me!" Ruu screamed. She grabbed the pole and tried to take it into the hut. She threw it aside. She crawled inside and shouted, "Do you not care about the troubles we are having? Do you not care about our troubles? You are one of us!"

Kru whined, "I am sick."

"You are sick! There is more to this world than you. We are in trouble and you do not care. You care only about your troubles. You care only about yourself. You say you cannot help because you are sick. Yes, you are sick. Your life is sick. Your spirit is sick. You are sick because you will not help. The tribe—no—all you care about is yourself. There is only your troubles, only yours. Even if you solve your troubles, what difference will that make if we are all dead? Who will care then? What will your happiness be worth then? You say you are sick. You are wrong. You are dead. But you do not have the courage to die, nor the will to live, nor the heart to help. Go, die already! Your sickness is that you cannot feel anything beyond yourself. Die, die, you sick, disgusting—"

Ruu slapped her hard, again and again.

"You leech, you bloodsucker," Ruu screamed.

"That is enough," shouted Hsoro.

Ruu crawled out of the hut. She stood and spit at Kru. She clenched her fists as she walked away. She leaned against the stone wall and stared out at the meadow.

Shouting and high-pitched yelling cut through the village from over the knoll. The Tribe jumped to their feet and ran to the knoll. The children raced around the field, swinging their clubs and watching the ground. A young girl dropped club at her feet and, crying, buried her face in her hands. Others sprinted past her, dashing across the field, pounding the ground. An older girl screamed as she dove through the air with her club held in front of her. They both slammed hard onto the ground. Everyone stopped.

Some of the children bent over, panting. Others walked quietly toward the girl, lying still on the ground. A boy bent over her. Around her, the other children gathered. He lifted her club. He looked at the ground underneath it, then whooped. The children jumped up and down, clapping and yelling. They patted her on the back as she crawled forward. She lifted something from the ground and nestled it in the palms of her hands. She carried it proudly to the village. The other children, smiling and laughing, followed behind her. They walked to the hearth. In front of the fire, the girl laid down a tiny, dead mole.

The charred bark of a log cracked, then curled up into the blazing fire. Sparks burst as another log split loudly, exposing its soft white insides to the consuming fire. The fire crackled, the coals burned white hot, and the flames glowed intensely blue, and higher, bright red. Drops dripped down and the fire jumped up from the ashes. The flames flickered. The wind licked the fire. The fire licked the meat.

Into the wind swirled the soothing smell of wood smoke and the wonderful aroma of roasting elk. The soft pink flesh, turning on a spit of its own bone, browned over the hearth. Fat, sweating through the pores, basted the slick, glazed skin, and then, slid off and dropped down into the fire. Searing flames slapped at the glistening, wrinkling flesh. Droplets of blood drooled from the shriveling veins. Warm, succulent juices oozed as the golden-brown skin bubbled, blistered, and burst. Small globs of crusted fat sputtered and sizzled. Cracking and crinkling, the meat sighed and hissed and shrank away from the scorching flames. Blackening at its knee and haunch, the charred skin of the leg rolled back into itself.

The men and the children walked to the stream carrying empty clay jugs. They brought back the jugs filled with cool water. Mre filled a basket with acorn bread, fresh and hot from the oven. Sra carried a basket filled with raw wild onions and mustard greens. From the storage hut, Tya and Clata carried a large wooden tray and, on it, a large stone knife. They laid the tray down in front of the hearth.

The Survivors stopped, started looking around at each other, then stared at the empty place in the circle in front of the hearth. Rhae had always sat there, slicing and serving the meat. In the long silence, they listened to the crackling fire and sizzling meat.

Broda pulled his crutch under his armpit and stood. He hobbled around the outside of the circle. Behind the empty place, he stopped. He stood with his head down for a moment, then stepped in. Broda knelt and picked up the knife. Sra and Mre lifted the meat off the poles and laid it on the tray. Broda checked the edge of the knife with his thumb, then bent over the meat. He slit through the skin. The hot juices burbled out and onto the tray. Broda licked the juices off the knife. He turned to Jascha and smiled. Jascha smiled and nodded back.

Broda sliced into the leg. With each slice, the smiles on the faces of the Tribe grew and, so too, their eagerness. Their hungry eyes widened. The rich aroma of roasted meat filled the air. The Tribe could hardly wait for the meat to fill their empty bellies. They passed around warm loaves of acorn bread. Mre filled a bowl for Traro and placed it next to her. Broda sliced deeper into the leg. Sra filled a bowl for Kru and put it next to her. They passed around bowls loaded with meat and topped with wild onions and mustard greens.

They held their bowls in the palms of their hands, then set their bowls down in front of them. They took a piece of meat, tore it in half, and handed a piece to the person sitting on each side of them. They laid the pieces of meat on top of their bowls. The Survivors joined hands and bowed their heads.

Klena said softly, "Thank you, our fellow being, for the sacrifice of your life. Without your life, we, your friends, could not live. Without your death, we, your kin, could not eat. We will forever revere your spirit as your flesh fills us."

The Survivors raised their heads and looked toward Jascha. He bent over and picked up a piece of meat. He lifted it to his opened mouth. His stomach growled noisily. He looked down at his stomach, covered his lips with his finger, and shook his head, smiling. The children laughed. Jascha opened his mouth again and dropped in the meat. His throat swelled as the meat slid down. He grinned and nodded. The feast began.

Tongues licked expectant lips. Impatient lips smacked together. Hands slapped and rubbed together, then picked up the first pieces of juicy meat. Some sniffed the mouth-watering aroma of the steaming meat. Others leaned back, opened their mouths, and the meat disappeared down hungry throats. They patted their bellies, rolled their eyes, or stretched out their arms with long drawn-out sighs. Heads nodded, then bent back down over their bowls. Teeth bit down hard into large pieces of savory meat. Sharp knives slid by slick lips, slashing through big chunks of meat held tightly between clenched teeth. Swift hands ripped apart the tasty flesh and stuffed it into eager mouths. Slippery fingers tore the meat before gulping it down. Chins, shiny with grease, bobbed up and down. Saliva drooled down the sides of their mouths.

Teeth gnashed together. Chewed quickly, large hunks of meat slid down straining throats. Water spilled down thirsting throats. Juices dripped from their mouths. Grease slathered over their faces. Blood dropped on their furry hides. Hairy sleeves wiped their faces. Greasy hands rubbed against their hide-covered thighs. Hands scraped against the insides of emptying bowls. Outstretched hands held out empty bowls. Bowls, handed around, were filled and refilled. All the browned meat was cut away. Now, the meat was red, almost raw. No one slowed.

Great gulps of water washed down the meat. They burped and belched. Some stood up and staggered sluggishly to the latrine, carrying their bowls, not missing a bite. Others waddled to the stream, drank their fill, filled their jugs, and then, hurried back. Broda walked slowly to the latrine. On his way back, he picked up the bowl for Kru and took it to her hut. With the top of his crutch, he pushed the bowl inside. He did not hear anything, but did not stay to listen. He still felt hungry and hurried back to the feast.

Sweat flowed down their foreheads as they crammed more meat into their mouths. Long, stringy hair stuck to the sides of their mouths. They pushed it aside once or twice, then ignored it. They gnawed hard at the tough meat, then swallowed it with loud gulps. Onions and greens crunched in fast-chewing mouths. More meat was cut; more eaten. More greens were eaten. More water was drunk. Bowls were passed quickly to Broda. He stopped filling his bowl, loading the bowls, then his mouth, then the bowls, then his mouth. Greasy hands rushed into packed bowls, pushing more food into already full mouths. Water, grease, and blood flowed together down the front of their hides. Matted hair from their hides clung to their fingers, mixed with the food, and were shoved into opened mouths. The last loaf of acorn bread, ripped to pieces, disappeared into gaping mouths. The last bits of meat, picked off their laps, were licked off their fingertips.

Broda scraped the thighbone clean. "Does anyone want more?"

Stooped heads concentrated on cleaning their bowls.

"Here," he said to Mre, "this is for Traro." He handed her the tray.

"I will save it to surprise him when he comes home." Mre smiled and took the tray.

Broda took the bone. He laid it on the ground. He took a rock and, with it, tapped the bone along its length, cracking it. He grabbed the two sides and split it open. The thick marrow that had given life to this bone, he scraped out and put into his bowl. With a bowl of honey, he passed it to the children. They dipped the delicious jellylike marrow into the sweet honey. The children, although full, always loved their favorite dessert.

Lowered heads swayed wearily with dull eyes staring into empty bowls sunken deeply into tired palms. Bowls, scraped clean, slipped from slippery hands and clunked as they dropped to the ground and rolled clumsily on their sides before tottering over. Drooping jaws, with mouths hung open, let labored breathing and moans wheeze more easily as fingers picked clean clogged teeth. Glutted bellies, aching and straining against their confining skin, jutted out heavily. Exhausted arms fell to their sides and dangled limply. Heavy-lidded, bulging eyes stared blankly into the fire as the Tribe rolled on their backs and sides, succumbing to the stupor. They slid heavily into their own fullnesses. Their world felt thick and slow. Lounging lazily on the Hearthland, the Survivors rested in a world that felt easy and full of peace.

CHAPTER 29

"Uhh," Clata groaned as he got up. He walked to his hut and took his spear. As he came back by the hearth, he bent over and picked up the bowl filled with meat for his father, then kissed his mother on the cheek. He walked away from the village.

His full belly made him feel large and confident as he walked on the familiar path through the woods. "It feels good to have food in my belly. I would have liked to have stayed with the rest and fallen asleep, but Father must be tired of guarding the village by now. He probably wants to rest, too, and I want to prove that I can guard the village as well as anyone. I want to prove that I am no mere boy. My eyes are keen. My ears are sharp. I can walk so quietly that no one can hear me. I am as clever as anyone. I am good at hiding." He jabbed his spear into the air. "I am good with my spear. Nothing can get close to me before I get close to it and I can find anything before it finds me. This is my home. The forest is my friend. What I cannot guard, she can. She will not let anything hurt me and I will not let anything hurt her."

Clata crossed Small Creek. Ahead of him rose a small hill. On top of the hill, he could see the back of the familiar deerskin hide of his father. It covered a squatting form staring out over the forest. It did not move.

Clata often tried to sneak up on his father. He rarely got within ten strides before his father, usually without even turning around, called, "Clata!"

At the bottom of the hill, Clata knelt. He put down the bowl of meat. He grabbed his spear with both hands. He stayed low to the ground as he crept up the hill, stopping every few strides. The deerskin hide did not move. He crept closer. He could scarcely contain his pride when he stopped ten strides from his father. His heart pounded excitedly. Silently, carefully, he crept closer, one, two, three, four, five strides. He stopped again.

"Five more strides. This is good. I must be quiet."

He knelt on the ground and watched the hide. It did not move. It did not rise and fall with normal breathing. Clata moved a stride closer. His smile faded. He turned his spear and jabbed its blunt end against the hide. The hide did not move. The back of it felt stiff. Clata dropped to the ground. He jabbed it again harder. The shaft slipped in his sweaty palms. The hide slipped down, uncovering a rock. He crept up to the rock and knelt in front of it. A shadow crossed his feet and rose against the rock. Clata grabbed his spear and whirled around.

"Nothing moves quietly through the forest in autumn."

"Father!"

"What are you doing here?" asked Traro.

"I brought you food."

Traro looked around, then asked, "Where is it?"

Clata, too, looked around, then stopped and scratched his head. He jumped up. "I left it at the bottom." He dropped his spear and ran down the hill.

Traro laughed and put down his bow and quiver. When Clata returned with the bowl, Traro, still laughing, held the spear of his son.

"Thank you," said Traro, taking the bowl from Clata and handing him his spear. "You did well. You are getting better." He slapped his son on the back. He sat down, leaned his back against the rock, took a piece of meat, and ate it.

Clata sat across from his father and asked, "Where were you?"

Traro did not look up from his bowl. He pointed to a maple tree, waved his hand up, then pointed to an upper branch. He picked up another piece of meat and ate it.

"Whew!" Clata gaped at the high branch.

"I heard you coming," said Traro with his mouth still full. "You are quiet. My father used to tell me that when I came through the forest I sounded like an angry moose."

They both laughed.

Traro stopped and scratched his head. "I thought I was quiet." He looked over at Clata and said, "You are quiet." He dropped another piece of meat into his mouth.

"Let me guard?" asked Clata.

"No, there is no need."

"You need sleep. You must go hunting tonight. I am no boy. I can guard as well as you can."

"Hm!" Traro, acting slightly insulted, raised his head and his eyebrows. "You can guard as well as I can?"

"Well, almost," Clata answered. "Please, let me guard. You need sleep."

Traro ate another piece of meat, nodded his head, and said, "You are right, I need sleep." He leaned toward Clata. He stared at his son, then asked, "Do you know why I am here?"

"You are guarding the village."

"Do you know what I am guarding the village from?"

Clata lowered his head as he answered, "No, not exactly." He raised his head and looked at his father. He straightened his back and said, "But I am not afraid."

Traro smiled as he put his bowl down, leaned over, and laid his hands on the shoulders of his son. He pulled him close and whispered, "I do not know what I am guarding the village from."

"Then what should I look for?" Clata asked, trying to sound calm.

"Everything. Nothing. I do not know." He gripped the shoulders of his son tightly in his powerful hands. Traro felt Clata trembling as he held him closer. In a serious voice, Traro said, "Those who live in fear, do not really live. Do not be afraid, my son." Traro loosened his grip and his shoulders slumped as if a great weight had been lifted from him.

"Father, you are tired. Please, go home."

"You are right, Clata. I am tired. I will go home." Traro picked up his hide and covered himself. Clata picked up the bow and quiver of his father and handed it to him. Traro put the quiver over his shoulder and took the bow in his hand. He took the bowl in his other hand, stood up, walked a few strides, then stopped and scratched his head. He turned around, said nothing for a while, and just looked proudly at his son. "Do not be afraid," he said. Then, smiling at Clata, he added, "but be careful." Traro turned away and walked quietly down the hill.

Jamu slept outside the hut of his mother. He lay on his side with his knees to his chest. His bare belly swelled and shrank as he slept quietly. A happy grin filled his face. His head rested on an oblong object covered with tan leaves.

Ruu stared at him with increasing curiosity. She walked over and knelt beside him. She shook his shoulder softly. He rubbed his eyes, stretched and yawned, then rolled over with his back to her. She shook him again, harder. He rolled onto his back and looked up at her blearily. He propped himself on his elbows. Ruu pointed to the ground behind him and asked, "What is that?"

Jamu quickly sat up, turned and grabbed the thing, and held it firmly in his hands.

"What is that?" she asked again.

Jamu yawned and rubbed his sleepy eyes, then shrugged his shoulders.

"Where did you get it?"

He squinted his eyes as he thought. His half-closed eyes opened wide and he smiled brightly as he answered, "I got it from Grandmother."

"From Rhae?"

Jamu tossed it up and caught it. He tossed it again, as high as he could. The dried leaves of the oddly shaped thing made it wobble as it tumbled down. It fell through his hands and dropped on his lap. He looked down dejectedly at it. His shoulders slumped. He said, "I am lonely. No one will play with me."

"Everyone is tired, Jamu. Someone will play with you later."

He threw it high up in the air, but when he caught it he did not smile. "When is Grandmother coming back?"

"She had to go away."

"Will she play with me later?"

"She had to go away."

"Will she come home soon?"

"She had to go far away."

"She is only in the Grove. That is not so far away. Does she not like me anymore?"

"She still likes you, Jamu. She just has other work she must do now."

"But I miss her."

"So do I."

He looked down at his lap, then tossed the thing up again. It fell through his hands and dropped on his lap.

"Did Rhae tell you what that is?"

Jamu, pouting, refused to answer.

Ruu leaned over him and more loudly asked, "Did Grandmother tell you what that is?"

"No." He hugged it tightly to his chest. His eyes filled with tears. "Grandmother does not want to play with me anymore."

"Please, give it to me."

He shook his head.

"Please, Jamu, give it to me. Grandmother would have wanted you to give it to me."

Jamu wiped his eyes. He wrinkled his face and frowned at her as he considered her request. With his elbow on his knee, he held the thing against his cheek, and leaned toward Ruu. He remained motionless, staring at her, examining her, subjecting her to his thorough scrutiny, carefully deciding. Then he shrugged his shoulders slightly and extended the thing toward her.

She took it with both hands and held it tightly. She bent down and kissed him on his forehead.

"I am lonely," he said, dejectedly looking at his empty lap. He turned away, lay down, and, sniffling, rolled onto his side with his back to Ruu.

She stroked his head and whispered, "Thank you, Jamu."

CHAPTER 30

From an upper branch of a maple tree, Clata could see far in all directions. From this high up, he could see the mountains beyond the valley. Trees grew on the sides of the mountains, but stopped below their bare tops. In the dim late afternoon light, the peaks looked gray, the same color as the thick low clouds brushing them. The mountains seemed to turn their shoulders toward the north as if already bracing themselves against another hard winter.

He checked the path on Broad Mountain. He could see it clearly until, at the bottom of the mountain, it turned away from the ravine and into the white-trunked birch and aspen trees.

At the far end of Summer Valley, two paths separated at Tumbling Falls. One crossed over White Mountain. The other led more safely into Winter Valley. The Survivors used that path to go to the Cave.

He leaned out and searched the path beside Walking Stream. The path was empty. He stopped and stared at the trees that grew in straight rows in the Grove. The path continued. It cut across some open ground, then into a ravine, and over Small Creek. It cut across more open ground, then faded into the birch and aspen woods. The village was hidden beyond.

Clata smiled. He imagined himself an owl, up on his perch, watching the world around him. How wonderful it must be to see this far always. He felt happy. He was sure that he could see anything before it could see him or threaten the village. He was confident that he could guard as well as anyone.

Something moved through the woods. Clata leaned forward and squinted. The leaves of the maple tree blocked his view. He leaned out farther. Something moved on the path through the woods. It came from the village. Clata lay flat on his belly and crawled out the branch. Behind a birch tree, it stopped. Clata gripped his spear and waited. It moved again. It came to the end of the woods. Holding a long stick, it dug into the open ground, stooped down, and picked something up. It dropped something into a bag it carried. It came across the open ground, then down into Small Creek. It stooped again. The ravine hid it. Clata stood on the branch. It looked down into Small Creek. It took its long hair and pushed it away from its face. Clata smiled. He nodded and whispered, "Tya."

Tya wiped the sweat from her face. Her hands felt stiff, but her face felt soft. She looked down again into the still pool. She felt self-conscious about her face. It looked too thin to her, too bony, and her nose stuck out too far. Looking into the water, she practiced smiling. With her eyelids up, she smiled broadly, like laughing, but that looked too big for her face. With her eyelids half-closed, a small smile made her look surprisingly womanly. That made her grin. A shy, warm smile reflected from the water. Leaning closer, she frowned at a pimple on her forehead. She pulled her fingernail toward it, then stopped and shook her head. She dabbed her fingers into the still pool and watched her face disappear into the ripples.

Tya grabbed her stick and stood. She pushed her stick deeply into the ravine. She bent down, dug out a groundnut with her hand, and dropped it into her bag. She walked away from the stream, staying in the ravine, carefully checking one side, then turned around, checking the other side as she walked toward the stream. Near the stream, she climbed out and foraged the open ground away from the village. With a grace that came with experience, she wasted no motions as she jabbed her stick in, dug out, and dropped groundnuts into her bag again and again. Back and forth over the open ground like a grackle hunting for insects, Tya gathered more groundnuts. Her eyes stayed down, focusing on the ground as she moved farther away from the village.

Back near the stream, she stopped and, wiping the sweat from her forehead and rubbing her sore shoulders, leaned against her stick. She looked up the path toward the village, then along and down the stream. She looked up at the small hill. On top of the hill, she could see the back of the familiar deerskin hide of Clata. It covered a squatting form staring out over the forest.

She walked to the hill, laid her stick and bag down, and took out two groundnuts.

"Clata," Tya said softly as she reached the rock at the top of the hill, "I brought you some groundnuts."

Clata jumped from the tree and shouted, "Boo!"

"Oh!" Tya screamed.

A single red leaf fluttered down between them.

"Klena!" Ruu shouted through the village. "Klena? Has anyone seen Klena?"

Groggily, from inside his hut, Broda yelled, "He is probably sitting by the pond again."

Ruu ran to the top of the knoll and shouted toward Teardrop Pond, "Klena!"

"Over here."

Ruu ran toward the pond. "Klena?" she shouted again.

From behind the trunk of a willow tree, Klena waved his hand.

Ruu stopped beside him.

Sitting on the ground with his legs crossed, he leaned quietly against the trunk of the tree. He looked out over the surface of the gray water. As he watched, a gust of wind from the north rippled the smooth surface of the pond and the reflections of the trees on the far shore disappeared. Rubbing the scar on his forehead, he stared at the water. "How old is water?"

"I must ask you something," Ruu said impatiently, without looking at the pond.

Klena, staring at the pond, sighed, "It is so beautiful."

"I must ask you something, Klena." Ruu knelt beside him and lifted the thing she carried.

"Yes, Ruu, what do you want?"

She waved the thing in front of him and asked, "What is this?"

He took it from her and turned the thing over and over in his hands. He laid the thing on his lap. "Where did you get this?"

"From Rhae!"

Klena quickly looked over at her. His amber eyes widened and his face turned pale. "Rhae! You have seen Rhae?"

"No, I haven't seen her. Jamu had this. He said he got it from Rhae. What is it?"

Klena leaned back against the tree and smiled. He looked out over the pond, then up at the gray clouds filling the sky. He lifted the thing over his head. "Thank you, Rhae."

"What is it?"

He brought it down and turned it over again and again. His grin grew. He pulled off one of the husks. With his thumb he wiggled off three of the seeds, one yellow, one red, one black. He placed them on the husk. "These are seeds. We called them kernels." He held the thing gently in the palms of his hands. "This is corn."

"Corn?"

"Yes, corn." He leaned his head against the tree. His voice sounded warm and happy. "I have not seen corn for a long, long time. It disappeared when so many things disappeared. It towered over me when I was a child. It stood so tall. It grew in the sunlight. It was green, a soft, yellow-green. It was a beautiful plant. Each stalk would have six or more ears like this. Around each ear, husks cradled them tightly. At first the husks felt as smooth as the cheek of a baby, but as the mornings got colder, the husks stiffened, protecting the precious corn within, protecting it from the cold. In autumn the husks dried and turned golden brown. From the top of each ear, golden threads flowed, blond like the color of your hair. Earlier in autumn than now, we would pick the ears off the stalks. To cook them we left the husks on, wet them, and put the corn into the fire. The husks would burn, but the corn came out golden and tender. With each bite, the juices would drip down. Oh, it tasted so good and sweet. A few kernels would burn dark brown. I saved the burnt ones for last. Some of the kernels stuck between my teeth and it felt like a reward when I finally pried them loose. We also dried the corn, hanging it until the kernels turned hard. Then, we ground the kernels into flour and made bread from it. Corn bread, um, that I will never forget. Corn, it brings back so many happy memories from my childhood. I have lived long enough to become a child again. This is a precious gift."

Holding the corn tightly to her chest, Ruu repeated as if dazed, "This is a precious gift."

Klena nodded as he picked up the husk with the three seeds on it, wrapped the husk around them, and put it inside his hide. He leaned back against the tree and looked out over the pond again. "Thank you, Rhae," he said softly.

CHAPTER 31

Clata chewed on a groundnut while Tya rested her head on his lap.
With his other hand, he stroked her face. "You are so beautiful!"

"No, I am not!" Tya blushed every time that Clata told her that.
She covered her face with her hands.

"Yes, you are!" Clata smiled as he pulled her hands away from her
face. "You are beautiful!"

"No, I am not." She blushed again.

"You are the most beautiful woman in the whole world."

"Oh, Clata."

"Am I handsome?"

"Yes," she answered, smiling at him.

"Am I the most handsome man in the whole world?"

"Oh, Clata, this is embarrassing."

Clata finished the groundnut. He took both her hands in his and
looked into her eyes. "You are the most beautiful woman in the
world and I am the handsomest man. We must be the most beautiful
couple in the whole world."

"I do not know," she said, smiling shyly.

"I know we are. We must be. And we will have the most beautiful
children!"

"When the time comes," she added quickly.

"Oh yes, of course, when the time comes." He caressed her cheek
and smiled at her. "I will be a great hunter, even greater than my
father and grandfather."

"I am a good forager," she said, "and I will become even better."

"You must become the best forager in the tribe, even better than
Rhae." He stopped at the mention of her name. "We must be able to
feed our children so they will grow strong and healthy and make us
proud as parents."

"They will make us proud if we are not too proud of ourselves."

"Yes, Tya." He kissed her on the forehead.

She held his hands. "Clata, there is so much we can do together."
"We can change the world!"
"When we are the leaders of the tribe, there will be no hunger, no
misery, no sadness."
Clata squeezed her hands. "Tya, we can do anything."
"We can make our dreams come true."
"We will make the world better."
"We will love each other forever."
"I love you, Tya."
"I love you, Clata."
They hugged each other. Their lips touched tentatively. She pulled
back and opened her eyes. His eyes were closed. She slid her hand
over his shoulder. More surely, they kissed again.

"Hsoro!" Ruu shouted, "Hsoro!"
He raised his head.
"Hsoro!" Ruu shouted again, sprinting to the ditch. She stopped
above him at the edge. "Do you know what this is?" She bent over
and waved the ear of corn at him.
Hsoro squatted in the latrine. He stared at the strange thing that
she waved at him. "A plant of some sort," he said, shrugging his
shoulders. "What is it?"
"This is corn!" she shouted.
"Corn?"
"Corn!" She jumped around, dancing, shouting, "Corn! Corn!
Corn!"
He smiled at Ruu and asked, "Where did you find it?"
She jumped down into the latrine beside him. "I did not find it."
"Who did?"
"Rhae!"
"Rhae?"
"That is what Jamu told me. He had it."
"Hm." Hsoro stood up and shook his legs. He squatted down
again and grunted.
Ruu went on, "Do you know what this means? We are saved. All
we have to do is take one of these little seeds, plant it, water it, and it
grows. Hsoro, it grows. In autumn, we pick it. It does not move. No
more worrying about the uncertainty of hunting. If we cannot kill
anything, we will not go hungry. Maybe we can capture some ani-

mals, feed them corn, grow them ourselves, then kill them. Do you
think we could?"

Unenthusiastically, he answered, "I do not know."

"Aren't you excited? We, the Survivors, can grow, too. We can be
well fed and healthy, with strong adults and children, many children,
and a permanent village, maybe, a town. Imagine it, Hsoro, we will
have stability, security, and abundance. We will have an abundance
of time, time to build, to expand, to prosper. We can bring back the
greatness that was once ours. We will be the leaders. We will make
the world better than before. Hsoro, this is the beginning. Are you
not excited?"

Downcast, he looked at the ground under him. "Why?"

"Why?" Ruu asked, shocked at his indifference.

Pulling up a handful of ferns, he wiped himself. He stood and
pulled up his breeches. As he threw a handful of dirt over the small
pile, he asked, "Why should we begin it again?"

"Why?" she shouted.

He turned toward her and quietly asked, "Why should we plant it?
So, the Survivors will grow, and prosper, and the children will grow
healthier. And more of us will grow, and more of us will need, and
more of us will want, and the children will come faster than the old
people die. Someday, sooner than expected, there are too many people and they need too much food. What nature gives us no longer fills
our needs. So, we must dig up more of the earth to grow more food.
So, we must drive the animals from their homes, and move rivers,
and cut down forests, and rip down mountains. We build fences
around pieces of land and call it ours. And more children live, grow
up, and have more children. Will they believe that the earth is here
only for them? Will they believe that only their needs are important?
They must have food. They must own more land. Then, someday
sooner than expected, someone wants a piece of land that belongs to
someone else. So, they fight. The losers die, or starve, or will fight
again until they win. The winners grow, and prosper, and must fight
again until they lose. And what about those who look ahead? While
they cry, they are laughed at, or ignored, or killed. Meanwhile, there
are still more, and more needing more, and more wanting more, but
no one wants to see where it will all end. No one wants to look ahead
because it is too frightening. But, Ruu, we do not have to look ahead.
We have seen where it will all end. We have been through it. We are

the Survivors. Who will the murderers be next time? War, or disease, or famine, or something we cannot even imagine? We know the murderers will be the same. We know because the murderers are us. Ruu, we are the children of the Devastation, dare we start it all again?"

"We will not make the same mistakes again!" she shouted.

"How many times have we heard that?"

"We can change!"

"Can we? We cannot know that."

"I don't need to know that, I can believe."

"I cannot believe, Ruu, I must know."

"Answer me, now, Hsoro, because I must know." She put her hand on her pregnant belly. With her other hand, she pointed the corn at him. "Should we plant it?"

Hsoro looked at Ruu, then the corn, then again at Ruu. "We will do what we must to survive," he said.

Ruu looked straight ahead, not at him.

He laid his hand gently on her shoulder. He could feel her shaking. "We will plant it because we must," he sighed.

CHAPTER 32

Tya and Clata, holding hands, walked down the hill. At the bottom, Clata picked a daisy and handed it to Tya.

She sniffed it and smiled. She kissed Clata on the lips. "I will take it with us to the Cave."

She picked up her bag. Clata handed Tya her digging stick. They hugged and kissed. As they parted, their hands slid away from each other.

Tya smiled as she walked. She felt good and full of life. Even the day, ending and sliding into dusk, felt fresh and alive. She turned around and looked at Clata. He leaned against the maple tree with his spear in his hand, watching her. She waved to him, then turned away. As she walked on the path home, she lifted the daisy to her face and sniffed it again. Her face exploded. A sharp crack tore through the forest. She crumpled to the ground. The daisy fluttered down.

Clata dashed down the hill. Something grabbed his ankle. Pain shot through him. He stumbled, then fell. His spear rolled away from him. He tried to kick the thing off his ankle. He could not. It gripped too hard. He turned and saw the teeth of the trap digging into his bleeding ankle. He turned and crawled on his belly, struggling to reach Tya. The chain on the trap pulled taut. He dug his hands into the ground. Tya, facing away from him, lay just beyond his fingertips. He watched the puddle of her blood spread over the ends of her hair. He watched her back rise and fall, and stop. He strained against the trap ripping into him. He could not reach her. He could not touch her. He could not watch, and buried his face in his hands.

Two men raced on the path through the woods. Behind them, the woods rumbled with stomping feet and shouting. With knives drawn and gripped tightly, they ran shoulder to shoulder until they reached the ravine. Hsoro hurried through the ravine. Traro hurdled it, then dove to the ground beside Clata. He covered his son with his body. He listened, but heard nothing except the crying of his son.

Hsoro saw nothing. He knelt beside Tya. He placed his fingers on her neck. He felt no pulse. He shook his head toward Traro. Traro lowered his head onto the back of Clata.

Shouting people ran quickly on the path. Mekla, carrying his spear, led them. He jumped down into the ravine and ran up the bank. Waiting for him at the top, Hsoro grabbed him. Mekla saw Tya lying on the ground. He tried to shove Hsoro away, push him aside, knock him over. Hsoro fell back, but held on to Mekla, hugging him. Mekla, shaking, looked down at his daughter. He dropped his spear. His body softened as he leaned against Hsoro. He laid his face on the shoulder of Hsoro and, hugging his old friend, began to cry.

Sra screamed. She ran quickly across the ravine. At the top of the bank, she stopped and screamed again, then covered her mouth with her hands. She staggered forward. Her hands trembled. Her eyes stared down in disbelief. She fell to her knees beside Tya. Mekla dropped to his knees beside Sra and laid his arm around her quivering shoulders. Sra lowered her head softly and laid it against the back of Tya. She heard nothing. She turned and looked up at Mekla, then buried her face in his lap and wept. Mekla hugged her and sobbed.

From across the ravine, Ruu glared. Her eyes were dry. Her fists were clenched.

Behind her, stood Broda, leaning on his crutch, shaking his head sadly, his eyes filled with tears.

Klena and Mre stopped the children before they reached the ravine. Jamu wanted to see what was going on, but turned around with the others and walked back to the village.

Traro and Hsoro pulled against the teeth of the trap clamped into the bleeding ankle of Clata. He pulled impatiently against the teeth, ripping more of his flesh. Krilu pulled on the chain, but could not pull it up and threw it down in disgust. Traro and Hsoro opened the trap slightly. Clata slid his foot out. He crawled to Tya, laid his head on her back, and cried.

Krilu dashed around wildly, then rushed up to the top of the hill. He jumped on the rock, waving his bow and arrow, yelling incoherently. He took an arrow, nocked it, pulled his bow back until it creaked under the strain, then in frustration and anger, shot the arrow high and deep into the forest at nothing.

Traro slid his arms under Clata. Clata pushed his father away and tried to stand on his own. His leg collapsed. Traro caught him and lifted his son into his arms.

Sra reached out and took hold of her daughter's hand. She caressed it softly as tears flowed down her cheeks. Mekla crawled to the side of his daughter. He slid his arms under Tya and lifted her.

With Tya cradled in his arms, Mekla walked home. Sra still held their daughter's hand. Behind them, Traro carried Clata. Everyone else followed, except one. Hsoro stayed behind.

Dying streaks of light fell through the woods, then dimmed and disappeared.

Standing on the shore of Teardrop Pond, Klena waited. Mekla laid Tya down at the feet of his father. Sra held on to Tya a moment longer, then reluctantly let go of her hand. Mekla took Sra by the hand. They walked to the village.

Klena knelt. He undressed his granddaughter. He lifted her and slowly waded into the pond until Tya floated in his arms. He untied her hair and spread it out on the water. He washed the blood off her. With the soft water, he bathed her face.

"Death takes us all," he said quietly. "Some, you take too soon, much too soon." His eyes filled with tears. "Why?" He started crying. "Why Tya?"

He lifted her from the water and waded to shore. Hugging her to him, he said, "We will always love you, dear Tya."

Traro and Krilu brought the bier for Tya. Klena laid her down gently on the soft boughs. Traro and Krilu lifted it and walked to the village. Klena walked behind them.

A fire glowed on the Ground.

CHAPTER 33

The somber grayness of dusk crept into the forest, brooding through
the branches, clutching at the trunks, crawling over the roots, grabbing the ground, and, for its time, it covered the whole of the world,
until a powerful, sullen darkness, like a silent wildcat, stalked into
the forest, swallowed the dusk, and fell upon the village and the
Survivors. In the gathering blackness, the tribe sat huddled together
in a circle on the Ground, around a sputtering fire. Flickering faintly,
the feeble light from the small flame barely touched the deep shadows of the grief-stricken faces. Their empty True Knots lay in front
of them on the bare ground. Other than hands moving slowly to wipe
tears from their eyes, they all sat still. Other than mournful sighs and
hushed whimperings, they all sat silent. A bitter wind from the north
moaned through the forest. The tiny flame shivered.

Jascha, the tribal elder, sat, wrapped in a thick hide. Motionless,
he stared into the fire for a long while, then he nodded his head
slightly.

Klena leaned over the fire and laid a dried twig into it. "We must
have more light. There is much we must discuss." He turned away
from the fire, toward Hsoro, and asked, "Have you seen it?"

"No," Hsoro answered wearily. "I have not seen it, but I have
tracked it."

Klena nodded as he looked into the fire. "Tell us what you know."

Hsoro paused and took a deep breath. "I do not know what it is."
He sounded sad and tired. "It walks on two legs. It is big. Its stride is
half again as long as mine. Its foot is twice the size of mine. It is
heavy. Its prints sink deep into the ground. It destroys what is in its
way. It crushes bushes filled with berries. It cares little for the other
animals. It kills more than it eats. It eats much, but much is left to
rot. It does not keep its home clean. That is all I know." He lifted his
head and looked at Traro. "Do you know more?"

"It uses metal traps." Traro shook his head.

Hsoro opened his pebble pouch. He emptied the pouch into his hands. He felt through the pile, then scooped it up and put it back into the pouch. He handed something to Broda. "Do you know what this is?"

It felt cold and heavy. Broda looked down at the small object in his palm. He rolled it around. It wobbled. He looked up at Hsoro. "Where did you get this?"

"I dug it out of a tree trunk where Tya died. I cut it out with my knife. It was dug in deeply."

Broda put it into his mouth and bit down hard on it. Bending toward the fire, he took it out. It was gray. He turned it toward the light. On its side, he saw teeth marks. He handed it to Klena. Broda wiped the sweat from his palms on his thighs. He shook his head from side to side. His voice trembled as he said, "I have not seen one of these since I was a child."

His head hung down. His voice could barely be heard over the crackling fire. "Many, many years ago, when I was a child, we had long metal tubes called rifles. These rifles shot a piece of metal very fast and over long distances. We used up all the metal that the rifles shot. The rifles rusted and we threw the useless things into Teardrop Pond."

Broda looked around the circle at each of the Survivors, especially the children. He stared longer at each of the children. He reached out to Klena. Klena handed him the piece of metal. Broda looked at it again, then closed his hand around it. His fist shook in front of him as he said, "This is a bullet."

A long, long while passed in silence. Each Survivor stared into the fire. The flickering fire made them seem to move, but no one stirred.

The tiny flame grasped a piece of wood. It shuddered for an instant, then disappeared. The red coals brightened a ring of smoke as it floated away. Klena leaned over, laid a dried twig on the smoldering coals, then blew. The fire shot up, taking the twig. Klena looked into the fire and said, "Why does it shoot us? We are not mean or cruel. We are in harmony with nature. We live as all others live. We are as we are. Why does it kill us? Why will it not let us live in peace?"

"Our choice is simple," said Broda, leaning closer to the fire. "We can run or defend ourselves. We live here in peace with the forest, the streams, the animals. Now, we must fight. If we do not defend ourselves, it will not stop until we are all dead. This land is ours. We know our own land. We did not ask for this fight. But we must defend what is ours."

"What is ours?" asked Klena. "Our place in this world is a small place within nature. We are nothing without nature. How can we own the sky? How can we own the earth?"

"What we must have," said Broda, "we must defend. We do not simply want this land, we need it. We must have it. It gives us water, game, fruits, vegetables. We are rooted to this land. It is here that we must grow or die. This land will not be ours, if we do not defend it. This Other is dangerous. It kills us. We have no choice. It must be killed."

"There is enough space for all of us to live in peace," said Klena. "The earth is large. There are horizons upon horizons. We are a small people in a small place. If this Other wants the whole earth, why does it need this one small valley? One small valley? It cannot need everything. Nothing needs everything. If it lets us alone, we will live in peace."

"We have always stayed in our land. Animals are free to come and go if they do not take what we need or try to harm us. This Other does not leave us in peace. It wants more than a piece of our land. It wants the heart of our land. It wants to tear the heart out of us. My heart is mine. If I, Broda, cannot defend myself, I will rip out my heart and bury it in our land. This is where my heart belongs."

"What are we trying to prove?" asked Klena. "Our eyes are blinded by our anger. The land goes on and on. There is more land than we can ever need. New lands, stretching far beyond our narrow horizons, beckon us. We can fight and be killed, or we can leave this place and live. We will find new lands and hunt its game and raise our children and laugh and sing and grow old and die in peace. Let us leave this place and explore."

"We are a people," Broda pounded his chest and said, "we are the last remnants of our people. We must respect those who died so that we would survive. People have always stood, and fought, risked their lives, and died, so that their people would survive. They knew that there are causes greater than a single life. They knew that there must be sacrifices. They were willing to die for their people. Dare we dishonor their sacrifices now?"

"If we see a fight coming and run from it, are we cowards or wise?

Let us look wisely at this Creature," pleaded Klena. "It has cruelly
killed an old woman and a child. Can we kill like that? It has killed
without respect for other living beings. Can we kill like that? It has
killed and left their flesh to rot. Can we kill like that? We have seen
enough of its killings. How many more of us must die? What have we
become by sacrificing ourselves? We have become only dead. It is
more important to survive. Living is more important than victory."

"There is never enough for a Beast that wants what it does not
need," said Broda. "This Beast wants what is ours because it is ours.
If we go to another valley and it wants that, do we run again? Soon,
nothing will be ours. Not even our shadows. We will hide in the
darkness covered with fear until the end of our days. Our children
will grow afraid of the light, scared that someday something will
come again. It wants us to hide and cringe and live like frightened
savages. We live in peace with our world, taking no more than we
need, giving back what is not ours, living in harmony with the give
and take of nature. This Beast wants only to take and take. We have
barely enough as it is. We may not have enough to make it through
the winter. This Beast can take no more. Either we kill it or it will
kill all of us."

"My child is dead," said Sra, wiping her eyes, "she cannot be
brought back." She looked at the faces of the children. "But what of
the other children? Will they be murdered by this Beast? Will they be
killed for living in their homes? Will they live their lives worrying
that something out there is going to kill them, while they die inside
themselves? Frightened children can learn nothing about themselves.
They will distrust everything, hate and fear everything. They will
love nothing. They will carry nothing but pain and horror with them
for the rest of their lives. If they cannot grow in peace, they will grow
in hatred. We must make the world safe for them. Our children are
our hope."

"All of us want to live longer," said Mre, "we should not be
ashamed of that. All of us want to grow more, to accomplish more.
Our lives are important to us. We live our lives as well as we can. I
will do all I can so that my family and friends, all of us, will live."

Klena looked up from the fire and said, "In spring and fall, the sun
moves and the leaves change. The animals move south and north.
The water changes to ice and back to water. The days grow longer
and warmer, then the days grow shorter and colder. The seasons

change, and so, we move. We pack our belongings, strap them on our backs, and we move. We are not trees that grow in one place. We are animals, and we must move to stay alive. Change is good for us. Why do we fear it? Are we too set in our ways to see this as an opportunity?"

"It is cold," said Broda, covering himself with his hide, "and it will get colder and colder. Winter comes. Where do we go? Beyond here, all is unknown. But, wherever we go, winter will follow us. We cannot outrun it. When we are caught, where will we stay? Where will we find food? How will we live? Do we want to die cold and hungry, far away from everything we know? We will no longer be a tribe, but wretched, greedy scavengers, rooting through the snow for a morsel of food, grabbing food from the sick, despising the healthy, distrusting and fearing, plotting, killing, and revenging, until the last of us freezes and starves and dies. Is that how we want to die?"

"If the forest caught fire, would we leave?" asked Klena. "This place is not safe. It has been our home for a long time, but it is not safe now. Whatever we find beyond the horizon will be different, but not so different that we could not survive there. Other animals travel great distances and survive. We have little to carry. What is truly important, we do not have to carry. We have our minds, our experiences, and our skills. These we can take anywhere. They are in all of us. We are not helpless. We need not fear the unknown."

Broda patted his stomach and said, "First, there is food. What are we without food? Nothing but poor desperate scavengers, with empty stomachs. What are we with empty stomachs? What do we learn and accomplish, what do we believe in? First, the stomach must be fed, then the mind grows sharp, the heart grows warm, and the spirit within us grows full. Our food is scarce, winter is coming, and the only thing growing is the hungry ache in our stomachs. If we do nothing, all of us are doomed to a hollow death of hunger. Already, there is not nearly enough food for this coming winter. This Beast has taken our food from us. It has taken what we desperately need and left it to rot. It is taking our way of life. It will starve us to death, if we do not stop it. The Beast must be killed."

"I do not know if we can kill it," said Traro. "It is big and strong. We can defend ourselves better from here. Let us wait."

"But we must get into the Cave," said Mekla. "If we do not get in, we will freeze. We must not wait. We must kill it."

"We must not underestimate it. That is foolish."

"We must not wait. That is more foolish."

"We do not know what it is. I do not know if we can kill it," said Traro, shaking his head.

"Everything kills," said Traro's father. "Everything on earth kills because it must eat. Nothing kills for the cruel pleasure of killing. This Beast does. It kills without respect. It is without love, kindness, or compassion. It must not continue on this earth. It will destroy everything we believe."

The rustling of leaves shook the silence of the circle. A dark form limped toward the firelight. Traro jumped to his feet and rushed toward his son. Clata weakly waved his father away. Slowly, Clata walked across the Ground. At the edge of the circle, he stopped, looked toward Jascha, and lowered his head respectfully. Jascha nodded his head in return. Clata took off his True Knot and laid it on the ground. His voice quivered as he said, "There is something my father and grandfather taught me." He stopped and took a deep breath. "They said," his voice grew stronger, "if you know yourself and are pure in spirit, and if you are prepared to kill and to be killed, when you must kill, you are within the ways of nature and there is no blame." Clata lowered himself carefully down.

"I am an old man," said Klena. "I do not mind being killed. But I would rather live by running bravely, than be killed foolishly. There is nothing brave in being slaughtered. It is foolish to walk into a useless death. What have we taught our children by walking into a slaughter? They will say, 'The men died foolishly. They did not use their minds. They let their anger control them, and they were killed. They left us alone, because they were foolish. They did not think about us but only about themselves. They would rather be killed and call themselves brave, than live and be called wise.' "

Broda said, "All beings defend what belongs to them. If they do not, they will be chased and hunted. Do we want to be killed far from here by this murderous Demon, this Demon whose only advantage is that it is evil enough to kill without thinking? Perhaps, we think too much. If we want to live, we must be ready to kill."

"Do we want to become like this Beast? What have we won when we must become like it to win? Any victory is empty. We become it by using its evil ways. Is it right to become evil to destroy evil? Dare we start down that way again?" asked Klena.

"If we do not defend what we believe," said Broda, "we are surrendering to its beliefs. We will have given in to a Beast that cares only for itself. If we do not kill it, the world will be overrun by this greedy, destructive Devil that murders without eating, kills without need, covets without end, and steals food from the mouths of hungry people."

"I am tired of the cheap talk of old women!"

Broda slammed his fist down hard and glared through the fire at Krilu. "Be careful what you say, young man, I am not too old to teach you respect."

Sitting away from the others, Krilu stroked an arrow. He stood, then stomped across the Ground. He stood over the fire and threw his True Knot in front of the men. Looking down, Krilu scowled at them as he said, "I am tired of the cheap talk of old men! Look at you! Here you sit on your behinds and you talk. It has murdered my mother and you talk. It has murdered Tya and you talk. You talk and you talk. Now, listen!" Pointing his arrow at the men, he shouted, "Revenge! It has killed, it must die. I want my revenge. I, Krilu, swear to you that my arrow will kill it." With the white quartz point of his arrow, Krilu picked up his True Knot and rushed away.

Ruu slammed her fist against her thigh and said, "We must do something! We are not what we think, or feel, or believe. We are what we do. It is a cold-blooded murderer. Its own kind must kill it or its blood will flow into its children. If its own kind shirks its duty and will not kill it, we must. What we think, or feel, or believe, does not matter. We must do what we must to survive. We cannot run from our responsibility." She slammed her fist down again. "It must be killed."

Hsoro picked up a handful of dirt. He opened his hand and watched the dirt flow slowly through his fingers. "I do not know what is good or bad." He spoke quietly, his eyes down. "I only know that there are those who survive and those who do not. The ones who survive judge what is good. We are the Survivors. We must judge." His head rose slightly as he took a deep breath, but his eyes never lifted from the Ground. "Anything that murders us is bad. We must survive." His chest and shoulders sank.

The end of his cane crunched into the Ground as Jascha pulled himself to his feet. His hide slipped off his shoulders and dropped to the Ground. Leaning against his cane, Jascha stood upright as he looked into the fire. "I speak not twice. Thou shalt not kill. It was written many, many ages ago. It was written and broken many, many times. They became empty words. Killing became common. Life became cheap. The old words hold true. Thou shalt not kill. That is how it must be. That is right. We must kill to eat. That is how it must be. That is right. Life is precious. It is wrong to waste life. Waste is wrong. Thou shalt not kill wrongly." He bent over, picked up his hide, wrapped it around himself, and turned away from the fire. Jascha walked into the night.

Silence filled the circle.

The last tiny flame from the fire died. Blackness filled the circle. No one stirred.

The glowing coals cracked and crumbled. They became dark and quiet.

Hsoro barely nodded his head and whispered to himself, "I know." No more was said.

CHAPTER 34

Huge heavy clouds, damp and full of ice, thick dark clouds, like an avalanche of floating boulders, tumbling silently against each other, covered all the world like a grave, devouring all the light of the moon. The north wind blew, pushing through the shaking woods, clattering and rattling the branches.

Shadows shivered wildly over the path like restless spiders.

Old withered trees, tangled and crammed together, formed an incomprehensible confusion of strange and grotesque shapes. Great sagging trees leaned over, choking the narrow path. Hiding in the shadows, briar bushes, bending low to the ground, seemed to crawl along in the blackness, nibbling and nipping at the edges of the path.

A squat shape, obscure but steady, with gleaming yellow eyes of a poised animal, lurked in the darkness.

A quick gust of sharp swirling wind picked up and threw the leaves, rustling them against each other and pulling more from the trees. The trunks of the trees groaned and sighed, and the branches creaked and squealed, then stopped.

A cone bounced against the side of a tree, hit the ground, hit again, then disappeared.

Lurching precariously from side to side, tentatively rising, then falling, the tiny path sank down, dodging the large boulders, twisting around the thick trunks, wriggling deeper into the intense blackness of the forest.

Slippery roots, like large snakes, slithered up from the broken earth, stretched across the damp dirt, then curled around and dug themselves into the dark ground.

Shadows shivered wildly over the path like uneasy spiders.

Willow trees leaned toward each other, nudging each other like bored old crones, pointing their spindly branches down at the trivial life at their roots. Worn maidenhair ferns, shuddering on the cold ground, dipped their heads into Walking Stream.

Licking weakly at the heads of the wilted ferns, the stream sounded faint and far away. The crunching of dead leaves drowned the dull pluck of a cone splatting into the water. The water pushed quietly against and around the wet rocks. The cone sank to the bottom of a still pool. Ice broke suddenly under the weight of a foot.

Creeping over the trees, blotches of thick moss gripped the trunks. A light, a glimmer of fluorescent light, glowed from the rotting trunk of a decaying tree. A squat shape, with the steady gleaming eyes of a poised animal, prowled through the darkness.

Rising straight and tall, two large trees covered the small path. From a group of trees, arranged in long, orderly rows, came a single anguished cry as handfuls of dirt dropped into the ground, filling a hand-dug, shallow hole. Cold water poured from baskets onto the dirt sounded somber and mournful. The gentle patting of opened palms on the wet dirt sounded empty and hollow. The dried leaves laid on top of the low mound covered, but did not hide, the fresh grave.

No words came from the choked voices of the Survivors as they knelt around the grave. No simple high-pitched flute melody was played. The women and children moaned beside each other with their hands over their faces to hush their sobbing. No reassuring low drumbeat was thumped. The men wiped the tears from their eyes as they watched and listened carefully for any movement that may betray its presence. Sharp, icy pricks of coldness stung them as specks of snow, falling through the branches of the apple trees, touched the shivering skin of the Tribe.

The Survivors paused for a moment over the grave, then turned, and walked away. They left the Grove. Outside, three men, holding their bows and carrying their quivers, and one man, with a sling and pebble pouch tied to his belt, turned away from the path that led back to the village. They walked away into the forest.

The snow kept coming and coming. The dark surface of Walking Stream glazed along its shores, around its cold rocks, and froze together into a stiffening layer of ice that the snow covered with a silvery sheen. The powdery snow drifted down through the trees, through the branches, off the leaves. The fragile flakes touched the ground and dissolved and disappeared until their coldness thoroughly overwhelmed the ground. The earth surrendered to the whiteness of the falling snow. The snow covered the bare ridge of White Mountain.

A lone howl joined another, then another, and another. The human-sounding chorus of long howls grew louder and fiercer, then tailed off into silence. The deep howls made the silence between them more melancholy and lifeless. Four dark figures gathered in a circle. They touched noses and sniffed, nuzzled each other and wagged their tails. In a single file, they set out again. The pack, hungry, determined, and persistent, stalked the bloodied prints of a wounded elk. The gray silhouettes of four wolves moved across the snowy ridge atop White Mountain as the long night brightened to morning.

As if all other life, held so dearly, was but an insignificant transient intruder, tolerated but ignored, trespassing in these timeless shrouded valleys with their tiny frozen streams and small frozen ponds, the forest, standing aloof from the eternal daily dance of life and death, the dark mysterious forest, silent and snow-dusted, stretched and spread and rolled on and endlessly on and on. The icy-tongued breath of another of countless winters sang through the pointed peaks of the old trees and older mountains. The incessant wind, from the north and biting cold, gripped the floating puffs of clouds and, relentlessly ripping and shredding, scattered and flung them over the horizons, like fluffs of forgotten lives, until all the heavens were empty. The earth was dead still. The moon drooped low in the sky. A last glimmer of starlight gleamed in the darkness of the west. And, once again, the golden sun glowed on the eastern horizon.

Fourth Day

CHAPTER 35

The sun rose over Unknown Mountain. Its cool light shivered down the bare cliff above Winter Cave. Three small figures, wrapped in hides, squatted on the narrow ledge. Traro leaned against his bow, an arrow leaned against his thigh, three more lay on the ledge. Mekla, in the middle, took an arrow out of his quiver and placed it in his bow. Krilu, with his arrow nocked, stretched his bow and pointed it down.

In the snow, on his belly, on the far side of the clearing, lay Hsoro. The sunlight trembled down Twice-a-year tree. The shadow of the tree reached across the clearing, darkening the mouth of the cave.

"Ahh!" From inside the cave came a disquieting groan.

Hsoro looked at the mouth of the cave, then up the face of the cliff. Three taut bows pointed down. He nodded his head. Traro and Mekla nodded back. Hsoro stared again at the mouth of the cave. He saw only blackness. He heard crunching on dirt. A vague form moved inside the cave. It disappeared back into the blackness.

Clutching his hide, Hsoro crawled cautiously forward. The cold wind rattled the bare branches of the tree. Snow dropped on him and pattered on the ground.

A dark figure came to the mouth of the cave, stopped, then went back into the blackness.

Hsoro lay flat on the ground, his heart thumping.

"Ahh!" Another groan came from the cave.

Hsoro shivered. His hands trembled as they crept down his side. He untied his pouch, turned it over, and rolled some pebbles into his palm. His numb hands could barely feel them. He looked down, picked out the heaviest pebble, and loaded it into his sling. He wrapped the sling around his left hand. The rawhide stuck to his sweating palm.

He looked up the cliff. The bright sunlight crept down toward the ledge. The three men waited. Traro turned and shielded his eyes against the line of light closing in on them. He turned and anxiously looked down to Hsoro. Hsoro watched the Cave.

Something came to the mouth of the Cave, stopped, then crawled out. It stood and groaned as it stretched. It walked away from the Cave. In its right hand, it held a rifle. In its left hand, it carried a piece of polished glass. It leaned its rifle against the cliff. It wedged the glass into the cliff. From a sheath at its right side, it pulled out a large knife. Scraping the blade against its face, it watched itself in the mirror.

It stood more than a foot taller than any of the Survivors. It was big and strongly built. Its large boots were of smooth, heavy leather. Its breeches were not of leather but of a dark blue cloth. They fit snuggly on its long legs. Its shirt was of thick cloth with red and black stripes. It pulled tightly on its broad shoulders. Its hair was light brown, thick and wavy, trimmed and combed.

Interested, Hsoro raised his head. He looked into the mirror. In the mirror, he saw a handsome face about the same age as his own, but golden-tanned and smooth, its forehead free of wrinkles. Its eyes were bright blue, the color of a clear morning sky. Its nose was small. Its lips were light pink. Grinning at itself, its teeth were white and even. Its cheeks were dimpled. When it finished shaving, it rubbed its hand over its face, admiring itself.

The face suddenly changed. Its eyes looked hard. Its hand tightly gripped the handle of the knife. It whirled around and looked straight at Hsoro.

Startled, they stared at each other.

Hsoro stayed still, but his heart jumped against his chest. He looked curiously at the creature. It looked back frightened. Hsoro watched it put its knife back into its sheath. The snow crunched as the creature took a slow, deliberate step to his right. Hsoro, his mind full of questions, stood and stared.

The creature quickly grabbed its rifle.

Hsoro tried to lift his sling. His left arm hung limply at his side. His hand quivered but did not move. His shadow stretched across the clearing and touched the feet of the stranger. Hsoro lifted his right hand and offered his opened palm.

Glowering furiously, the stranger lifted its rifle and fired.

Hsoro felt something hit his shoulder. The crack of sharp thunder exploded. His back slammed against the ground. Pain roared through his body. Blood flowed from his shoulder. His sling dropped from his hand. He grabbed his right shoulder. As he lifted his head off the ground, he watched the creature stalking angrily across the clearing.

The long rifle pointed at Hsoro and fired.

The bullet sliced across his forehead. His scream drowned the crack of the rifle. From the wound, blood slid down his face. Hsoro crawled away.

The creature, panting wildly, came forward. Hsoro, crouching, heard the click-click of the rifle bolt. Towering over Hsoro, the creature lifted its rifle and aimed. Its eyes were filled with hatred.

The sun, blazing over the top of the tree, blinded Traro. He squinted into the light reflecting off the snow, aimed, and shot. His arrow skimmed over the shoulder of the beast, missing it, but hitting the barrel of the rifle.

The rifle fired. The bullet buried itself into the ground by Hsoro.

Mekla aimed at the sound of the rifle and shot. His arrow struck the beast in its side.

It howled loudly, turned, aimed its rifle at the cliff, and fired.

The screaming bullet shattered against the cliff near Mekla. Sharp fragments hit Mekla and Traro. Traro, hurt, doubled over. His bow dropped off the cliff. He stumbled over the ledge. Mekla dove and grabbed him. Traro dangled over the ledge.

The beast aimed at them.

"No!" Hsoro yelled.

The beast turned and suddenly stared at Hsoro.

"Kill him!" Ruu shouted from the top of the cliff.

An arrow whizzed through the air. It tore through the back of the man. It ripped through his chest. Spurting blood sprayed the snow. Blood gushed down his chest. Blood dropped off the white arrow point.

He staggered. The swaying rifle pointed at the heart of Hsoro and fired. The bullet smashed into the ground.

He wobbled, leaned against his rifle, and straightened himself up. He took two ponderous steps forward, stumbled, then dropped to his knees. The rifle dropped from his hands. He reached out for it and plopped hard on the ground. The arrow shivered in his back. He groaned as he reached down and pulled out his knife. On his hands and knees, he crawled toward Hsoro. He reached out his hand and slashed his knife at him. The knife slipped from his hand and stuck into the ground. He clenched his fist, then fell into the snow. Blood, oozing from his chest, dyed the snow red before melting it. He lifted his head. He coughed, spitting blood. Squinting in the sunlight, blinking his eyes, he looked up at Hsoro, then collapsed.

Hsoro, drops of sweat shimmering on his face, crawled forward. Blood from his head and tears dripped down his cheeks. Blood from his shoulder soaked his arms and hands. He knelt beside the man. The back of the man rose and fell and rose as he wheezed. Hsoro bent down, his hands trembling. He gently stroked the face of the man. Leaning closer, their cheeks touched. His voice aching, Hsoro asked, "Why?"

The man dug his hand into the ground and lifted up a handful of it. "It's mine—all mine."

The dirt slipped from his hand.

The wind blew snow against their faces. Their breath blew across the earth together, then one stopped. The head of the man slid slowly through the hands of Hsoro.

CHAPTER 36

"YAA!" Krilu yelled from the ledge, his arms outstretched triumphantly over his head.

"Hsoro!" shouted Ruu, jumping up and down on the top of the cliff. She ran down.

Mekla pulled Traro up on the ledge. They hugged each other. Mekla asked, "Are you all right?"

Traro rubbed his arm, smiled, and nodded to Mekla.

Mekla smiled and put his arm around Traro.

Krilu, waving his bow over his head, ran down the ledge. He jumped into the clearing and sprinted.

"YAA!" he yelled again.

He stood puffing over the corpse. He stepped on its back and pulled his arrow out. He circled Hsoro and the corpse, prancing and brandishing his arrow.

Traro walked up behind Krilu and patted him on the back, then looked down at Hsoro.

Hsoro stared at the fallen man.

Traro knelt beside Hsoro. He put his arm around his shivering friend. "How are you?" he asked softly.

Hsoro just nodded slowly. He still stared down at the man.

Ruu ran across the clearing. She dropped to her knees beside Hsoro and hugged him.

He did not move.

Mekla came from the Cave. "There are piles and piles of furs," he said. "Why so many?" He carried a leather belt filled with shiny bullets.

"I do not know," Hsoro said slowly.

Mekla put the belt down.

Hsoro turned to Ruu and said, "Please leave. Go and tell the tribe that we move."

"But—" Ruu interrupted.

"Go," he shouted. "Go!"

Hsoro stood. He walked around the man. He picked up the cold rifle and threw it at Krilu. "It was your shot. This is yours."

Krilu grinned as he stroked the rifle tenderly in his arms.

Hsoro grabbed the bullet belt and threw it at Krilu. It smacked Krilu across the chest.

"We are saved," Krilu yelled, wrapping the belt around his waist. "Now I can kill anything!"

Hsoro, his eyes glaring angrily, turned to Ruu. "Take him and go," he shouted. "Now!"

Frightened by his look, Ruu stepped away from Hsoro. She looked to Traro. Traro looked at Hsoro. No one spoke. No one dared to argue.

Krilu stared defiantly at Hsoro, then raised the barrel of the rifle. Ruu grabbed Krilu and dragged him away. She pushed Krilu ahead of her as they ran up the cliff face. At the top, they stopped and looked down.

"Go!" Hsoro shouted.

They turned and disappeared over the top.

Hsoro looked down at the man. He bent down and rolled the man over on his back. Hsoro closed the eyes staring blankly up at him.

Hsoro unbuckled the belt and loosened the top of the pants. Traro lifted the legs of the man as Hsoro pulled off the pants. Leaning over the chest of the man, Hsoro unbuttoned the shirt. Traro lifted the head of the man as Hsoro took off the shirt. Hsoro carefully folded the clothes and laid them in a pile.

The bloodstained body of the man lay naked on the white snow. Hsoro looked at the hands of the man. He lifted the left hand. He pulled a gold ring off the fourth finger, then stared at it in his palm. He slid it on the forefinger of his left hand. It fit.

Hsoro unsheathed his knife.

Traro grabbed him tightly by the wrist. He pulled the knife from Hsoro and laid it on the ground.

Hsoro looked up at Traro.

"Do not be sad, Hsoro. We did what we must."

"We must survive," said Hsoro, "and we must change ourselves now."

Traro took the metal knife from the ground and handed to Hsoro. The knife felt cold to Hsoro. He turned it slowly until its sharp edge faced himself. He slid his thumb over the edge. The cut on his thumb filled with warm blood. Hsoro gripped the handle firmly.

He knelt over the corpse. His fingers slid down the breast bone. When he reached the softness of the upturned belly, he stuck in the point of the knife.

"I do not know about monkeys eating monkeys, but I do know about men eating men, for certainly all evidences of anthropology point to a pretty universal practice of cannibalism. That was our carnivorous ancestry. Is it therefore any wonder that we are still eating each other in more senses than one—individually, socially, internationally? There is much to be said for the cannibals, that they are sensible about this matter of killing. Conceding that killing is an undesirable but unavoidable evil, they proceed to get something out of it by eating the delicious sirloins, ribs, and livers of their dead enemies. The difference between cannibals and civilized men seems to be that cannibals kill their enemies and eat them, while civilized men kill their foes and bury them, put a cross over their bodies and offer up prayers for their souls. Thus we add stupidity to conceit and a bad temper."

Lin Yutang

ABOUT THE AUTHOR

Bruce Stolbov was born and raised in the Appalachian Mountains of Pennsylvania. His extensive background in anthropology, ecology, primitive religions, and psychology provides the solid foundation for *Last Fall.* Stolbov lives in San Francisco, California. This is his first novel.